SILVER CHIEF

SILVER CHIEF
TO THE RESCUE

BY
JACK O'BRIEN

Author of
Silver Chief, Dog of the North
Valiant, Dog of the Timberline
Alone Across the Top of the World

Illustrations by KURT WIESE

THE JOHN C. WINSTON COMPANY
Philadelphia
Toronto

F 1249

THIS BOOK
IS
DEDICATED
to
DONALD AND PETER

CONTENTS

CHAPTER   PAGE

I. The Race of Mercy 1

II. A Well-earned Rest 20

III. A New Friend 42

IV. Under Suspicion 60

V. Hitting the Trail 80

VI. A Shot in the Back 100

VII. Pursuit 117

VIII. The Capture 136

IX. On Trial 153

X. Out of the Bush 183

XI. Homeward Bound 204

XII. The Last Assignment 221

LIST OF ILLUSTRATIONS

Silver Chief . . . . *Frontispiece*

PAGE

The Mounty opened fire, and three shots whipped
out in quick succession . . . . *facing* 8

They swung off the frozen watercourses and were
toiling up the bank 15

Silver Chief brought the gauntlets back to Jim . 29

Together they stalked ptarmigan, flushed rabbits,
investigated the scent of caribou 65

Baker pointed to the west trail 93

The powerful jerk spun him about so quickly that
he dropped to the snow . . . . *facing* 105

Mickey had caught up with them 107

Back of him came the team . . . . . . *facing* 120

Suddenly Silver Chief stopped short and swung
his head around 127

PAGE

He started across the snow on his hands and knees 143

"What a fool I've been," Thorne muttered to
  himself 177

At last they reached Eskimo Point 189

The dogs romped on the beach 215

1

THE RACE OF MERCY

A SILVERY bubble puffed up from the coffeepot spout, slid down its side, and burst in a hissing cloud of steam on the hot stove. Winship doused half a cup of cold water into the pot to settle the coffee and shoved it to one side. Then, hearing outside the slow crunch of footsteps against the snow, he drew from the oven a pan of hot bannock and a skillet of gravy-drenched deer steaks.

The door opened and closed quickly on the burly figure of a man. Without speaking, he placed his small, black case on a bench near the wall and slowly pulled off his heavy coat, moving as if his limbs were weighted with lead.

Winship set the food on the plain board table beneath the glaring gasoline light. Then, turning back to the stove, he spoke without looking at the newcomer. "Things any better tonight, Doc?"

Doctor Meade drew a sweater off over his head and hung it on a wall peg. From a boiler on the stove he filled a basin and carefully washed his hands. Not until he stood drying them on a rough towel did he answer Winship's question.

"I'm afraid not, Dan," was his reply. "If help doesn't come soon, I'm about at the end of my rope."

Winship poured the coffee, placing the steaming cups beside the food, and pulled up two chairs to the table. Wearily the Doctor lowered himself into one of them. For several moments he sat staring at the dishes spread out before him. Winship, too, sat down but neither man attempted conversation nor began to eat. Outside the wind whimpered at the window like some hapless traveler from another world seeking entrance to the warm room. The wood in the cookstove crackled fiercely and then dropped against the grates with a melancholy rattle. At last Winship picked up his knife and fork.

Dan Winship, Manager for the Hudson's Bay Company, although younger than his companion by many years, had lived long enough in the North to know fatigue when he saw it. Meade *was* near the end of his rope, and as Winship ate, he pondered uneasily how he could best prevent the Doctor from breaking under the strain, for he knew that Meade would go on until he dropped. Between bites Dan studied him, noting the mechanical way he plied his knife and fork as if he hardly knew he were eating. Under the white light of the overhead lamp, the Doctor's round, ruddy face was etched with deep lines of exhaustion and his eyes held an unnatural brilliance as of fever, belying the fatigue which showed in his every movement, in the sag of his body as he slumped in his chair, in the effort with which he moved his hands.

"How long have you been in the North, Doc?" Winship sought to divert his friend's mind from the troubles that confronted him.

"Thirty-five years," was the answer after a moment's hesitation. "Came up as soon as I got my degree from McGill."

Dan looked at him in amazement. "What in the name of heaven made you pick this blasted section of the world to carry on your lifework? You could have had a good practice somewhere, with all the comforts of civilization, an office, a car, a telephone . . ."

Meade reached mechanically for another helping of steak. He seemed to be groping for a reply. Then he shrugged his shoulders helplessly. "What are *you* doing up here? You're young. Life's just beginning for you, and yet here you are. Well, I came for the same reason, wanting something different, wanting to be a part of something new and big, wanting to help those who have the courage to break away from the ordinary world and reach out for new horizons. That's why I came. And I've stayed because it gets in your blood and then you can't break away."

Meade sighed. "Sometimes I do wonder what it would be like to have a nice, clean office with nurses to help me, to make my calls in a car instead of slogging along for miles beside a dog team. Clean linen, clubs, companionship. But those are dangerous thoughts to a man in the bush, and now that I'm getting older, they don't come so often."

He stopped and drank deeply from his cup, and as he set it down, a slow smile lighted his face, the first sign of relaxation that Winship had seen in him for days. Leaning back in his chair, Meade held a match to his cigarette.

"But don't mistake me," he went on. "I wouldn't trade this life for anything in the world. I've stood in a battered old cabin with only a sputtering candle for a light and, with my hands blue from cold, pulled a man out of the grip of death. Or maybe it was a woman. Or a fine baby struggling for life. And when I see the look of thanks that glows in their eyes, it pays me back for everything I've missed. No, Dan, they can have their city practices and their fine hospitals and fancy clubs where they sit around and tell each other how great they are. Give me the North. This is where I belong."

Winship helped himself to more coffee and touched off a smoke. It was true. White man, Indian, or Eskimo, they all looked alike to Meade. They all received the same ministrations. Not one of them had ever called in vain in his hour of need. Across the thousands of miles stretching from Hudson Bay to Coronation Gulf, from Great Bear Lake to Coppermine, he was spoken of in terms of deepest affection and respect. When the call went out for "The Doctor," everyone knew that, come freeze or high water, his call would be answered, for something stronger than his professional obligation bound him to these people. He was their friend.

It was because of such a call that he sat with Winship tonight. A little group of his widespread family was suffering and in need. Diphtheria, the horrible scourge that had once before raged through the land, leaving a terrible toll of death in its wake, now stalked the silent wastes again, and Lake Caribou lay gripped in the choking clutch of the disease. Twenty families made up the community, a population of thirty-five whites and eight Indians. And already five stone-heaped mounds lined the brow of the hill near the river. Ten other cases had developed, four of these among the Indians, who were always most susceptible to the white man's illnesses.

Meade had been found at Pendleton, eighty miles to the north where he had just arrived with the intention of wintering there. An Indian runner traveling by fast dog team had brought him word of the stricken village, and the Doctor had hurried down the frozen watercourse of Big River.

Aided by only the crudest equipment, he had plunged into the fight with a desperation born of love as well as of duty. Night and day he had worked unceasingly to stamp out the relentless advance of the black death that struck its victims with such startling swiftness, leaving them clutching swollen throats with trembling, fever-parched fingers, until at last their agony was relieved by merciful suffocation.

Three deaths had occurred before his arrival. Two others were so close to death that his untiring efforts could not save them. Yet despite the poor facilities, the lack of serum, the inexperienced assistance, the Doctor had gone from cabin to cabin and had managed somehow to slow down the advance of the dread disease.

But heart and will can accomplish only so much. Without the serum the Doctor could ease the suffering of his patients but he could not much longer stem the rush of the plague. Day after day Winship had tapped out the message for help. Day after day there was no response, and the Doctor was beginning to crack under the strain. Sleeping only two or three hours in every twenty-four, snatching a bite of food when he could, usually as tonight at midnight, exerting every bit of knowledge he possessed to help his people— all these things were beginning to exact their price. Without the serum Winship knew that the Doctor could not hold out much longer. Without the serum he must fight a losing battle.

Meade shoved his cup over to be refilled. "Is the generator still working all right?" he inquired anxiously.

"Yes, thank the Lord. There's plenty of gas and the motor's new. No need to worry on that score. I've been sending out the Churchill and Chesterfield call letters all day, but they're so far away it looks hopeless to expect help from them even if they catch the signals. Our only hope now is that Padley or Eskimo Point may tune in while I'm on the air and pick up the message. They're amateurs and only get on when they have nothing else to do, but they could reach us quicker than anyone else."

The Doctor stirred his coffee wearily, his eyes fixed on the dancing flames that licked out of the open firebox of the stove. "Little Mildred Baker is worse tonight. Fever 103 and a dangerous-looking throat. And there's Stroud and Henderson. Neither of them shows any gain, and I'm positive Mrs. Walters will be down before morning. Poor woman. She's worked so faithfully with me. I don't know what I'll do without her."

Suddenly he leaned across the table toward the other man. "Dan, in all my experience I've never been afraid when I was on a job. But this time I am desperately afraid that this thing is going to beat us. And I'll have to stand here day after day and watch these poor souls suffer and die and not be able to do a thing."

He banged the table with a resolute fist. "Dan, we've got to get that serum. I know you're doing everything possible, but keep on doing it. Hammer away at that key every minute you get. Never mind what hour. Somebody may be listening in." He turned away, his courage gone as suddenly as it had come and despair taking its place. "Someone has *got* to hear us."

Winship's pity for the man sounded in his voice as he replied, "I'll keep at it, Doc. You can trust me. But you stretch out here and get some sleep. You can't go on this way forever. What will we do if you cave in?"

THE MOUNTY OPENED FIRE, AND THREE SHOTS WHIPPED OUT
IN QUICK SUCCESSION.

He spread a blanket carefully on the bunk close to the stove. "Come along now, and let me make you comfortable. Then I'll clean up the dishes and get on the air. Maybe tonight's the night we'll get through." He laid a hand on the older man's shoulder, but Meade shook his head and tipped the ashes of his cigarette into a saucer.

"Thanks for the offer, Boy—and for your encouragement. It helps. But the Indian, Louie, is in a bad way, and I haven't seen him for several hours. Maybe after that I will lie down for an hour or so. But when I do, I can't sleep. Not with all those people on my mind."

He drummed the table with his knuckles and in a low voice as if he were reproaching himself, said, "If only there was something I could do. If only I could get that serum somehow—anyhow."

Winship shook his head and turned to stoke the fire. It was past one o'clock and the wind had increased, whipping down the chimney to send the sparks whirling in wild dances up the flue. Meade sat at the table and smoked over a third cup of coffee while Winship put away the food, scraped the plates, and put them in a pan of hot water. Rolling up his sleeves, he washed the dishes and set them on the table to dry.

At last the Doctor ground out his cigarette and rose slowly to his feet. Dan watched him as he walked across the room.   Meade put on his hat and coat and pulled on his mittens.   "I'll make just two calls," he promised, "and then I'll come back and try to get some rest."   Picking up his case, he went out the door.

There was no moon.   Overhead millions of stars glittered frostily, looking so near that the Doctor felt he could reach up and scoop them out of the sky with his hand.   The first banners of the Northern Lights played majestically across the heavens, long tongues of red and yellow and green.

The dim outline of Big River was just visible, winding down across the Barrens, while close to its bank, darker than the night, stood a grove of spruce, an inky clump against the whiteness of the snow.   Cabins lined the river banks, their flickering lights gleaming yellow in the blackness, and as Meade walked toward them, he thought how ominous they appeared, like the baleful eyes of a pack of lurking animals.

It was cold, savagely cold.   The fresh stirring of the wind drove the stinging frost deep into his flesh. Before he had gone a hundred yards, the Doctor was forced to throw his arms across his face to keep his nose and cheeks from being frozen.

The shabby cabin which he entered first was badly lighted and disorderly.   Through the sharp, medicinal odor, there pierced the unmistakable smells of smoked meat and tanned skins.   A battered lantern stood on a packing case beside a roughly built bunk. Deerskins formed the covering of the bed, and beneath their grimy folds lay a dark-eyed, dark-haired man, his copper skin an ugly, feverish red. Beside him sat another Indian, dressed in heavy woolen clothing and moccasins. He looked over his shoulder as Meade entered but he did not rise.

The Doctor put down his case and came to stand at the bedside. He took the sick man's hand in his, feeling for the pulse. The Indian's eyes, fever-glazed and brilliant, searched Meade's hopefully. The Doctor took a thermometer from its case and slipped it beneath the man's tongue. Resting his hand on the burning forehead, he spoke to the Indian who sat in silent attendance.

"Lots of cold cloths on his throat and lots to drink, as much as he wants. If he can sleep, it will help."

The Indian nodded and dipped a towel into a basin on the floor. As Meade left, he looked back from the door and saw the Indian bending over his brother with the fresh, cold cloth.

The next cabin was neat and well kept, but the atmosphere of terror was as oppressive as it had been in the Indian hovel. A motherly, gray-haired woman came to the door as Meade entered. She took his hat, case, and mittens and managed a brave smile of greeting, but her face was wan and drawn. She knew that if her baby could be saved, this man would do it. Near the stove sat her husband, a huge man, tanned from long days on the trail, and wearing the clothes of the country, moccasins, "stagged pants," and heavy checked shirt. He nodded a somber greeting to the Doctor and turned back to his task of tending the fire and boiling the water for tea to warm them through their cold, nightly vigil.

The trouble with these people, Meade thought, was that you couldn't get them to leave their families once they were stricken. It made his work doubly difficult, because the disease was so easily transferred from one to the other, but deep within him he loved them for their fearless devotion.

The wasted figure of a pretty, curly-haired little girl lay on the bed in the corner. Meade was pleased to see that she slept, although her flushed face and labored breathing were still as pronounced as they had been earlier in the day, and her throat was badly swollen. Silently he worked over her, the anxious mother at his side anticipating his every move. There was no need for words. All three knew that everything possible was being done. They could only hope and put their trust in Providence.

When the Doctor left, he pressed the woman's hand. "Keep up your courage," he said. "The serum may come tomorrow, and we will save her."

But it was a courage that he could not feel himself. Wearily he turned his steps toward the Trading Post Store. He was so tired that it was an effort to lift one foot and set it down ahead of the other. As he entered Winship's room, he saw that the rawboned, red-haired manager was bent over his radio table at the far end of the room, ceaselessly tapping the key of his instrument, stopping only now and then to drink from the coffee cup at his side. Dan nodded toward the pot of hot coffee on the stove and went ahead with his signals.

Ta-da-dit—ta-da-dit—ta-da-dit—ta-da-dit. Over and over again the skilful fingers moved swiftly up and down on the key as the call letters for Churchill, Baker Lake, and Chesterfield swirled out upon the frosty air to flash north and south their urgent cry for help.

The Doctor sat on the edge of his bunk and sipped his coffee. When he had finished, he removed his outer clothing and stretched out on top of the blankets. For nearly an hour he lay staring at the logs of the ceiling, the staccato hammering of the call letters pounding through his tired brain.

Ta-da-dit—ta-da-dit—ta-da-dit—ta-da-dit. Please send help, please send help, please send help. Meade found himself setting the words that were in his heart to the rhythm of the radio call. Please send help.

please send help, please send help.   For days now the plea had been going out across the frozen wastes. Must it be in vain again tonight, he wondered.

At last Winship snapped off the switch and pushed back his chair.   "That's two hours at ten-minute intervals."   He stretched his long legs and yawned. "No use trying any more tonight, but I'll get on the first thing in the morning."

Later as they lay in the darkness and listened to the moaning wind, Meade spoke in a voice that was thick with fatigue.   "The Baker youngster is going. If she lives through another forty-eight hours, it will be a miracle."

For a long time Winship did not answer.   There was nothing to say.   He tried not to think of the anguish that Maude and Jack Baker would feel if they lost the little girl they loved so dearly.   "Get it off your mind, Doc," he said finally.   "Try to get some sleep."

Dawn.   In the east the black sky was slashed with a long, crimson slit that widened moment by moment. And at the first early streak of light Winship was up and at the sending key.   He divided his attention between tapping out the signals and preparing breakfast.   The tangy smell of bacon aroused Meade, who had managed to drop off for two hours' sleep.

Breakfast over, the fight against death began anew. Craig and Stewart, two trappers, came to the Store to

THEY SWUNG OFF THE FROZEN WATERCOURSES AND WERE
TOILING UP THE BANK.

report that their partner, Reynolds, seemed worse. Meade hurried away with them. Then he visited the Baker youngster and the Indian. After that he made the rounds of those whose condition was not yet critical. Such people as were able to be about came to the Trading Post to make their meager purchases and to inquire about the sick. Winship was kept busy all morning waiting on them and working the radio.

A strange silence hung over the little camp, an ominous silence, heavy and tense. Death was in the air—death and fear. Heavily clothed men and women huddled in little groups before the cabins, talking in low voices. Meade moved from one cabin to another seeming to grow older and more careworn as the day advanced.

At noon he stopped long enough to eat a little food with Winship who had kept faithfully at the task of sending out their need of help. The condition of the sick remained unchanged. Midday rarely brought about a crisis. It was the night and the early morning hours that they had all come to dread

Darkness shut down early. At three-thirty the sky's gray deepened into purple. Long shadows traced their patterns through the spruce groves, and in the north the Aurora glowed like the lights of some far-off, enchanted city. Winship had just finished splitting and carrying in the night's supply of wood when the door of the Store burst open and Jack Baker burst into the room.

"A team, Dan," he shouted breathlessly. "There's a team coming up the river. Maybe it's help at last." Then he was gone to spread the news.

By the time the Manager had hurried into his parka and reached the outside, a crowd was pouring into the little clearing before the Hudson's Bay Store. Some of the men were running toward the river bank where a giant team of huskies raced swiftly across the crusted snow with a heavily loaded Alaskan sledge. As Winship appeared, they swung off the frozen watercourse and were toiling up the bank.

Trotting beside the sledge, his hand on the "gee" pole, the driver, clad in frost-spangled furs, called out suddenly to the big lead dog. The leader wheeled instantly and trotted to the door of Winship's store.

"Whoa—whoa—Boy!"

The driver swung his weight on the pole and dragged the sledge to a stop. The team dropped in their tracks, red tongues dripping, sides heaving. Doctor Meade pushed his way through the excited crowd and threw his arms about the shoulders of the driver.

"Thorne—Jim Thorne. Lord, man, but I'm glad to see you. You've brought the serum?"

The big man nodded. "Right."

Meade slapped the newcomer on the back while Thorne laughed and tried to pull away. Then, still holding him by the arm, Meade turned to Winship. "This is Sergeant Thorne of the Royal Canadian Mounted, Winship. Jim, meet Dan Winship, the Manager of the Hudson's Bay Store here." The Mounty and Winship shook hands.

Then the Doctor pointed to the beautiful, gray dog who lay stretched out upon the snow at the head of the team, his watchful eyes noting his master's every move.

"And there, folks," the Doctor said to the crowd with a happy smile, "is the greatest dog in the North, the only one who could have made this run and got here in time. This is Silver Chief."

II

A WELL-EARNED REST

THORNE stood chatting with Dan Winship. The
Doctor moved to the sledge, and as he yanked
loose the lashings, he called over his shoulder:

"Come on, boys, let's get this stuff into the Store.
We've got work to do."

Thorne stepped up beside Meade. "Here. I'll
help. You'll find the medical supplies on the front
end. My stuff is all stowed near the back."

There was no need to call twice for volunteers.
Eagerly the happy people shouldered the bundles and
hurried with them into the Trading Post. There
Meade ripped open the packages marked "Medicine,"

his experienced eye quickly singling out the carton containing the serum. Before the men had finished carrying in the load, he was at work mixing the solutions and then was off, moving from cabin to cabin with the life-saving antidote.

The Mounty had left his own gear on the sledge, waiting to be directed to his quarters. As Winship helped him to readjust the lashings so that they would hold temporarily, Silver Chief lay quietly on the ground at the head of the team watching them. The Manager looked at the great, gray animal admiringly.

"Man, that's a real dog you've got there," he said. "Where under the sun did you get such a beauty?"

A grin creased Thorne's face. It pleased him to have people admire the Chief.

"I picked him up about three years ago in the West," was the answer. "I was out there on a job that kept me in the bush all winter. This chap kept nosing around my cabin every night. He was full of fight and inquisitiveness. The first time I saw him I knew he had wolf in him, but I wanted him just the same."

Thorne grinned reminiscently. "Believe me, it was some job to catch and break him, but once he got the idea that I wasn't going to hurt him, that I wanted to be his friend, he fell for it, hook, line, and sinker. Can't get the beggar to let me out of his sight now."

He seems to consider that he was placed on this earth with only one mission in life, to look after me. Come along. I'll introduce you."

The two men walked toward the front of the team. Head tilted and ears erect, Silver Chief watched their approach with a questioning expression. The Mounty squatted down and took the dog's muzzle between his hands, stroking the soft fur and rubbing the little depressions behind the ears. When he spoke, it was as if he addressed a child.

"Nice going today, Old Fellow. Tired, aren't you? Fifty-six miles we covered and never a change of pace. You sure kept the rest of those muggs on the jump, didn't you?"

An answering growl rumbled deep in the dog's throat and one paw came to rest on the gloved hand of the man who patted him. The dog's eyes, grave and soft, glowed with the happiness he felt at this praise. But as Winship dropped down beside Jim, the growl changed to a threatening grumble and the neck fur bristled. Thorne tightened his grip, but the dog's eyes turned toward the man who knelt beside his master.

"Steady, Boy, steady," came from Thorne as he continued his petting. Aside to Winship he said, "You're new to him, that's all. Just don't make any quick moves until he's used to you. He's jealous of any stranger who comes close to me."

Thorne continued to talk in a low, even tone as he gradually loosened his grip on the dog's jaws. Silver Chief's head swung sharply toward Winship and with lowered nose, he sniffed cautiously, watching him closely as he drew slowly nearer.

"All right, Old Boy, go ahead," Jim advised. And to Winship, "talk to him. Let him hear your voice."

Winship spoke, dropping his voice to the pitch of Thorne's. "Easy, Silver Chief. Easy, fellow."

After a moment Jim said, "Now move your hand slowly off your knee and hold it out to him."

Carefully the other man followed instructions. At first Silver Chief drew back and looked at Thorne. But Jim said nothing and the dog turned again to the extended hand, moving his nose toward it. At last, after a series of poking movements at the steady hand, he seemed satisfied that all was well and held quiet as Winship rubbed his ears.

"Shake hands, Chief," was Jim's next order. Instantly the great paw was lifted and placed in Winship's hand. Dan shook the paw several times while the dog's head drew back with an air of aloofness as if to show that he accepted these liberties at his master's insistence but still preserved his own right to be wary of the newcomer.

"You're in," Jim said to Winship as he rose and straightened his shoulders. "He never shows much emotion, so don't misunderstand if he doesn't make a fuss over you the next time you meet. But he's got you pegged and he won't forget you."

Winship stood beside the officer, still watching the dog. "He's a champ all right, Sergeant. What will you take for him?"

Jim's laugh filled the air. "Your life and a million dollars. Now tell me where I am to live."

Winship pointed to three cabins which stood along the slope of the hill rolling back from the river. "Take that end one. It's new and I think you'll find it comfortable. There's wood in the back, and if you need anything, just shout for it. After you get squared away, come down to the Store for supper."

"Righto." Thorne went back to the sledge and gripped the "gee" pole. A single word of command brought the team up standing. Another shout and Silver Chief swung sharply to the right, leading the way at a racing pace until they stopped before the log hut which Winship had indicated. The Mounty moved his luggage inside and set the lights to burning. He started a fire and put on kettles of water to boil. This done, he came out carrying a small ax. But before he went into the grove to prepare the beds for his charges, he walked over to the team to begin the usual ritual performed each night after a hard day on the trail. From wheel dog on down the line, Whitey,

Corky, Prince, Firpo, Red, Angus, Krimbo, and Mike, each came in for his share of petting and good-natured roughing, and each responded with growls of happiness and clumsy clawing at the master's hand with big, shaggy paws.

Then Jim went on to the grove. He picked out the smallest trees, those whose branches spread close to the ground, and these he trimmed off to a point about three feet above the snow. The smallest twigs were nipped off the limbs and trodden into the snow, forming a soft mat, dry and warm. He saw that many trees near by had been trimmed and around them was evidence that other dog teams were being picketed here. They were probably out on the trap lines now, he reflected, as he brought the dogs and chained each husky to his place. Farther back in the grove he could make out the shape of a roughly built kennel. Soft whimperings came from it and the occasional short, angry bark of a puppy. A mother husky must be cuddling her litter there.

That day's run had tired his dogs, and Thorne knew by the way they sank to their brush beds that they would not relish food until they had rested a while. With Silver Chief at his heels, he returned to the cabin and set the place in order. He cut nine hunks of caribou from a quarter and took eight of these out to the team. Rested now and eager for food, the eight

3

dogs came to their feet, straining at their chains as Jim went down the line, tossing their food between their paws. He stood watching them for a moment. Then he spoke to them.

"Eat hearty, my lads. It's a lucky thing for you we got here tonight because that's the end of the meat. It's fish and bran for you from now on unless we can knock over a caribou in the next day or so."

Back in the cabin, he gave Silver Chief the remaining hunk of meat. Silver Chief retired to the deerskin which had been spread in the corner for him and began to eat.

The big lead dog was the only one of the team that had never been picketed. In the early days after Thorne had first captured him, it had been necessary to keep the Chief close at hand while he was being trained, and as time went on, the dog took it for granted that his place was with his master day and night. His was a double job, leader of the team and Thorne's bodyguard. At first the Mounty had worried about this for he feared that the dog's insistence on staying indoors with him might soften him for the trail. But such fears had soon been proved ground-less. No matter how long they might be detained at Detachments, and there were often weeks at a time when he never touched a harness, once they hit the trail again, the Chief was always the strongest and swiftest of the team. The rugged constitution that he had inherited from his wolf father gave him a stamina unequaled by the others.

Thorne stripped off his trail clothes and hung them on a wall peg. From his duffle bag he took out underwear, socks, fresh moccasins, khaki shirt, and heavy, blue, gold-striped uniform breeches. Then he bathed and shaved as best he could with the hot water from the kettles. When he was dressed, he made tea and sat on the edge of his bunk smoking and sipping the welcome brew.

An angry chorus of barking broke through the stillness, and both the officer and Silver Chief hurried to the door. In the light of the flaming Aurora whose reflection shimmered off the snow, Jim could see that another team had arrived and was being greeted by his dogs. As Thorne watched, he saw the driver lift a bulky load from the sledge. Caribou probably. He closed the door and returned to his tea. Silver Chief followed, squatting on his haunches before his master.

"Did you see that, Old Boy?" Thorne said to him. "There's meat in the land. Meat. Understand?"

The dog cocked his head to one side as if trying to puzzle out the meaning of the words. "Tomorrow," Jim went on, "you and I are going out and get some of it. Now bring me my parka and gloves. We dine out tonight. Gloves, Chief."

The dog whirled and trotted to the center of the room.   He looked about and then headed for the table where he raised up on his hind legs, grasped the fur gauntlets lying there, and brought them back to Jim.

"Parka," was the next command.

This was lying across the back of a chair, and the dog, gripping it as carefully as if it were breakable, fetched it as he had the gloves.   Then he stood back proudly and watched Thorne put them on.   A friendly pat on the head, the lights turned out, and the two of them went out the door into the brittle-cold, brilliant night.

At the Store Jim found Winship and Meade.   The Doctor, just returned from a round of calls, was dousing his hands and face in a basin of water.   He turned a dripping face to the newcomer and called out, "Toss off your shawl and rubbers, Jim, my boy, and drag up a chair.   Dan will have the grub dished up in a few minutes."

Thorne hung up his outer clothes while Silver Chief stood sniffing the warm air, laden with odors of roasting meat, stewing vegetables, and freshly baked biscuits. At a word from Jim, the dog walked to a corner and lay down.

Meade scrubbed his shiny face with a towel.   "I'm delegated to convey the thanks of the camp to you, Jim," he said.   "You'll have a lot of folks falling on your neck in gratitude—as soon as they can stand up."

SILVER CHIEF BROUGHT THE GAUNTLETS BACK TO JIM.

Thorne's grin was embarrassed. "No need to thank me, Doc. It's enough for me that now they'll be able to pull through. I just happened to be the guy who was there when the call came through."

The Doctor laughed and turned to Winship. "Quite a modest shrinking violet, we have here, eh, Dan? He just happened to be there. Of course he didn't have anything to do with sledging full-speed to get that serum to us, or figuring out how it could be done at all. Say, when do we eat?"

"Coming right up, Doctor." Dan followed his answer by bringing the plates of steaming food to the table.

As he drew up a chair, Jim inquired, "What's the situation, Doctor? Have you got it in hand now?"

Meade helped himself to the meat. "It's a bit early to be sure, but I believe we've got it licked," he replied. "Little Mildred Baker is the first to react definitely. She's past the crisis. The others I can't be sure of for a few hours. Mrs. Walters, who has been acting as my nurse, is with them now." He attacked his plate with vigor. "By George, this is the first time I've had an appetite for days. Try some of this roast, Jim. I don't know how a swell cook like Dan has escaped being married all these years."

During dinner the Doctor explained to Thorne the fight they had been waging since the epidemic had fastened on the camp. Thorne listened, marveling at the quiet fortitude of these simple people. When dinner was over, he and Winship cleared away the dishes and washed them while Meade made another round of visits. On his return he seemed entirely satisfied. Taking his place beside the others at the stove, he packed his pipe and nodded his head slowly as if to confirm his own thoughts.

"We've got it licked," was all he said, but the relief in his eyes spoke eloquently of his happiness. When his pipe was going, he rubbed his knees with the palms of his hands and spoke to Thorne.

"Well, Jim, it's your turn now. We've been so excited around here that I haven't had a chance to talk about anything but our own affairs. How have you been keeping since I last saw you? Let's see, it was in Regina, wasn't it?"

"That's right, Doctor," Jim answered. "It was three years ago when I was passing through with a prisoner and you had just got into town. You were having a touch of the high life for yourself, I suppose."

"High life, my eye," Meade retorted jovially. "I was getting together a medical unit to take into Great Bear Lake. My high-life days are all behind me. But tell me, how did you happen to get our radio call? Where were you? Come on, Jim, give us the story."

The officer lighted a cigarette. "There isn't much to tell. I'd been shifted over to Churchill some months back to investigate some Indian trouble. I'd finished the job and was just waiting around for the bi-weekly train when Reese, the government radio officer, caught your signal and messages and brought them to me. The problem was how to get to you in time. That had us stumped for a while because it was out of the question to try to sledge the whole distance. We'd be too late. I guess it must be all of seven hundred miles by trail, isn't it, Doc?"

The Doctor nodded. "Easy. Maybe even more."

Thorne went on. "We discussed every possibility and always came back to where we started. It was too far and we couldn't make it in time. At last the station agent in Churchill had a happy thought. He recalled the Lindbergh flight through this country some years ago and remembered that gasoline had been laid down in the summer prior to that flight by a supply boat that put in at Eskimo Point, Baker Lake, Chesterfield, Coppermine, and Aklavik. And we thought there might be some of that gasoline left that they hadn't used. We knew, too, that the Northern Exploration Company was flying big planes into the Lake Nesbitt gold mining district three hundred miles south of Churchill. Now we were getting places.

"We got hold of Eskimo Point by radio and they confirmed the agent's idea about the gas. They reported that there was enough on hand to refuel a plane for a return flight—Churchill to Eskimo Point—but not enough to fly all the way in here and then back to Churchill. Then we got Lake Nesbitt on the long-distance phone and in five hours they landed a plane down on the bay for us. I loaded my gear and dogs and we took off. From Eskimo Point I sledged in. That's all there was to it."

"It's over three hundred miles from here to Eskimo Point, isn't it?" Winship wanted to know.

Jim nodded. "Three hundred fifty to be exact."

"How long did it take you to make the run?"

"Five days. We had good going."

The Doctor and Winship exchanged glances. They knew only too well the pace which Thorne must have set to make that run. He had averaged about seventy miles a day and they knew the North well enough to know that seventy miles a day was a hard pace, no matter how favorable the conditions were. The Mounty, however, quickly turned aside their attempts to sing his praises and pointed instead to Silver Chief.

"There's the guy who did it. All I had to do was try to keep up with him. The Chief seems to sense an emergency, and it's as if he knows I'm anxious to push ahead hard. The way he whips those other dogs along is something to see."

The big husky's head came up from his paws as Thorne spoke to him. "You pulled us through, didn't you, Old Timer?" A soft whine was the dog's only answer.

Winship had a question. "Sergeant, although I've been batting around the North for quite a few years, I don't pretend to know the first thing about sledge dogs. But from what I've heard and observed I always thought it was bad business to make a pet out of one of them. Spoiled him for the harness. And I've heard, too, that they were treacherous. How about it?"

Jim grinned. "I'll have to answer those questions one at a time. First, this matter of spoiling a dog. As a usual thing, that's exactly what happens. A sledge dog must be made to understand that his mission in life is to be of service, that he must spend his life in harness, serving man. He isn't meant to be a pet. It's tough on him, of course, because it's natural for any dog to be friendly and to want freedom. Take any puppy you've ever seen. Wasn't he the happiest, most carefree little cuss in the world? Well, you've got to correct that attitude from the beginning if you're going to make a good sledge dog out of him. You've got to ignore any overtures of friendship he makes. You've got to treat him rough. I don't mean that you have to be cruel. You just let him alone.

"As he grows older, he realizes that he's not to be pampered and he resigns himself to it. A human being is the same way. What you've never had, you can't miss. And that's the way it is with a sledge dog. Never having been shown affection or allowed his freedom, he doesn't expect it and he settles down to doing his best in harness. Once he's learned that hauling a sledge is his job, he usually takes pride in doing a good job of it. Oh, now and then you get a loafer, but you can always snap him out of it.

"But with Silver Chief it was a different matter. I've told you that he came to me out of the wild. And of course he's part wolf. The first job was to win his confidence. To do that, I had to let him live with me. It was necessary to impress on him that I was his friend, that I wouldn't harm him, that everything I told him to do was for his own good. Evidently he had been hurt or badly frightened by man, because for months after he came to me he would draw back swiftly if I made the slightest move. But as time went on, he came to believe in me. After that it was easy. It's natural for a dog to look toward man for protection and companionship. I must admit that I worried about the danger of softening him for a while, but I soon learned that he could lie around camp for weeks and then go out and run the legs off any husky in the North. And mine, too."

"But how about the other dogs in the team," Dan wanted to know. "Don't they resent his special privileges? Aren't they jealous?"

Jim laughed. "They may feel that way at first, but the Chief doesn't let them get away with it. Every time I have to get a new dog to replace one of the team, Silver Chief takes him out and conducts his own private investigation. To watch him, you would swear he was putting the newcomer through a series of questions. In the end Silver Chief usually has to give him a swell thrashing. After that there's no more trouble. If any of the dogs feel any resentment toward him, they are careful to keep it to themselves. They have learned that they're apt to live longer that way. The team I have now has been together for more than two years and they know better than to argue with the Chief. As a matter of fact, they're all pretty good pals; that is, as much as he'll allow any of them to get friendly with him. And they certainly do follow where he leads."

"But a husky is treacherous, isn't he?" Dan persisted.

Jim thought a moment before answering. "Well, Dan, as far as I can judge, they act pretty much as

you and I would.   Treat 'em right and they'll treat
you right.   Of course there have been instances where
a husky rared up a bit.   But if you'll investigate,
you'll usually find out that he had reason.   Maybe he
had been beaten up or mistreated.   As a matter of
fact, that happens oftenest when an Indian owns the
dog.   The average Northern dog hates an Indian like
poison.   He can smell one a mile away.   But I'll back
my dogs against any other kind in the world if they've
been given a fair shake.   Why, take the Chief, full of
wolf blood, as you know, yet when I'm home, he makes
a pal of my wife.   She can't move without that dog.
And I have a hunch it would be pretty hard on anyone who tried to harm her when the dog was around.

"As for the Chief's innate loyalty," Jim Thorne
laughed with affectionate memory, "you see a husky
here who is practically a deputy.   I'll have to tell you
some day about how we tracked a half-breed accused
of a killing halfway across Canada, and then had to
drive him back into camp while I suffered with a
broken leg.   Fellow named Laval.   He got sent away
to Stony Mountain Prison, hating the Chief and me
like poison."

The conversation shifted to the problem of food.
Thorne reported that he had seen one of the trappers
return with caribou, and that on his way in he had
noted evidences of both deer and fox.   The trappers

at Eskimo Point were having a good season, and the
Mounty felt sure that luck had turned for the people
at Lake Caribou.   The appearance of caribou was
always a good sign.

As Thorne prepared to take his leave, he made a
suggestion to Meade.   "Better let me go out with
some of the men and see if we can't bag some meat.
You need it, and I wouldn't be any help with the
nursing.   I'll take the Chief.   He's a fine hunter.   I'll
put him in with one of the other teams and let my
dogs rest up a bit."   And so it was arranged.

Walking home beneath the glowing Northern Lights,
Jim reflected on the honest simplicity and fineness of
these people of the North.   It was a wonderful thing
to see them patiently performing their part in this
great pioneer work, never complaining, always loyal
and straightforward.   Theirs was no easy life, controlled
as it was entirely by the caprice of nature, and yet they
accepted it cheerfully.   When the fur was plentiful,
there was happiness in the cabins and meat in the pots.

And their drab days were brightened by the few
extravagances that were possible, sweets and toys for
the youngsters, additional food supplies, ammunition,
and perhaps a bit of finery for the women.   But when
the season was barren, when the icy grip of the North-
land tightened during the long winter months, driving
the game from the land or sending it to burrow deep

into the dens beneath the drifts, then came the pinch of want and suffering, a suffering not understandable in civilized sections of the world where every need can be supplied by a trip to a near-by store.

Thorne considered himself an outsider for, although he had spent many years in the North, there had been long stretches when he had been on detachment outside the bush, far from these lonely outposts. These absences, as well as his occasional trips to the larger centers of Regina, Winnipeg, Edmonton, and Vancouver, made him realize that he could never belong here as did these people who had built their homes in this vast Northwest Territory.

Yet they were a happy people. They lived in their forsaken part of the world, raised their families, and went about their business without a thought for the troubled, greedy world outside. They were making history, Thorne thought, and some day people would be reading about them in books. He was glad that even though he must remain an outsider, he was here, sitting on the side lines, watching these pioneers build up their country.

It was a country, he reflected further, that hadn't even been scratched. Its wealth was tremendous. Airplanes were cutting down distances and easing the burden of transportation to the most inaccessible places. Radio brought the outside world to their firesides.

Thorne reached over and grasped Silver Chief by the front legs, drawing the dog upright to face him. Two heavy paws slapped down on the man's chest.

"This isn't such a bad world after all," Thorne said aloud. The Chief's head was tilted as was his habit when he was not exactly sure of his master's meaning. "Here we are in the midst of the development of what will one day be the richest country in the whole world."

The man pressed the soft jaws tight between his hands and whacked the dog's smooth sides. Then he dropped the Chief to the snow, and together they went into the cabin.

III

A NEW FRIEND

A LONG, cold nose jabbed Jim's face and a big paw scraped his arm. Morning had come, and Silver Chief was attending to his duty of rousing the officer. Jim stretched and put out his hand, a signal that he was awake. Then he jumped out of bed and started the fire. While the dog was having his morning run, Jim fixed breakfast. Over his second cup of coffee he spoke to the Chief.

"Today we'll take one of the other teams and see whether we can still use a 30–30 rifle. You'll probably have a lot of trouble with those fellows. I've never seen a trapper's team yet that could hunt. But you'll show them, eh, Boy?"

The Mounty had long ago grown into the habit of talking to the dog as if he were another person, and Silver Chief responded with his usual grave air of attention.

They got started early. Dressed in light wind-proofs and armed with plenty of ammunition, Thorne headed for the Store, Silver Chief at his side. Baker was there waiting to shake the officer's hand with a gruff word of thanks. His little girl was definitely on the road to recovery. Meade was busy organizing the men of the village to begin construction on new cabins near the one which Thorne occupied. As fast as the patients improved, they were to be moved into these huts, and the old germ-filled cabins were to be burned. Meade was grateful for Jim's offer to hunt food, as hands strong enough to do hard labor were few and meat was needed. Baker readily consented to turn his team over to Thorne and accompanied him to the picket line.

There was surprisingly little difficulty when the Chief took his place at the head of the team. The regular line-up was put into harness first. Then Jim called Silver Chief to the front. The regulars growled and one of them sprang at the big dog as he trotted toward the lead position. Silver Chief halted dead still in his tracks and eyed the brave one coolly.　Then he dove straight at the dog's shoulder, his jaws clamped into the flesh with a click, and the next instant the objector lay howling on the snow.　The other dogs watched with terror this cyclonic attack, dragging as far back from Silver Chief as their harnesses would permit.　But there was no need for fear.　He had administered his lesson and now trotted to the harness Jim held ready for him.　A few minutes later they whirled away toward the Barrens, Silver Chief leading at such a pace that any husky who might have still wanted to protest his position had no chance to stop long enough to make an issue of it.

The migratory herds of caribou in the Northwest Territory play a very important role in the lives of the people there.　The Eskimos use the skins for clothing, and the meat forms their main diet when they are inland away from the sea where walrus and seal are not to be had.　White man and Indian also use the caribou hides for wearing apparel because it is the lightest known fur that gives ample warmth and protection against the bitter Arctic cold.　Trail parties depend upon the meat both for human consumption and for dog food.

The caribou roam the trackless stretches of the Barrens in vast herds.　Although they are members of the deer family, they differ in one respect—they

are not quite so large as the moose of other sections of
the North. At times they band together in such numbers that it takes hours for them to pass through a
section of the country or to ford a rushing stream.
When they are on the move, the thunder of their
hoofs and the crash of their antlers can be heard
for miles. And while at times they appear in countless
thousands, at other times they disappear as completely as if their whole race had gone from the face
of the earth. Then comes want and privation.
Eskimos go ragged and hungry while white men,
warned by the scarcity of game, do not dare to under-
take long sledging journeys, knowing that to do so is
to court disaster. Self-preservation is the reason for
these mysterious disappearances of the caribou. They
have moved to isolated spots to find the tender moss
they love so well and to seek a breeding ground.

The coming of the caribou is a good omen, for not
only does it signify that there will be plenty of pelts
and meat, but it also heralds the coming of the fox.
This animal movement occurs in regular sequence and
its order is always the same. First come the caribou
herds, drifting across the lonely, wasted plains like a
huge undulating carpet of dark brown and muddy
white. They graze contentedly for hours, only rushing
in terrified stampede before the sinister, red-eyed wolf
packs which prey upon them, striking them down by

the hundreds.   After the wolves have glutted themselves on the hot meat, the clean-up brigade of fox
appear, to devour what the wolves have left.

Slinking across long, exposed points of land or standing on high, rocky cliffs, these cunning fur bearers
carefully sniff the air with their sharp, pointed noses
until they locate the spot of the latest caribou kill.
There they go to feed, and it is near these points that
traps are set for the catch.

Jim, who had had plenty of experience hunting
caribou with dogs, knew that only huskies trained for
the work could be used.   At least the lead dog must
be experienced.   The dog instinct was to rush headlong toward the herd the moment it was scented, which
startled the caribou and caused them to move away
so swiftly that the hunter could not come within
shooting range.   Silver Chief had been carefully
schooled.   His cardinal virtue, instilled in him since
the first moment Thorne had placed him in harness,
was to obey a command instantly.   This, coupled
with his implicit faith in the Mounty, made him
invaluable on the hunt.

They had traveled not more than half an hour when
Thorne noticed that Silver Chief's head was turning
repeatedly toward the west and that his speed was
slacking.   He must have scented the caribou.   Jim
brought the sledge to a stop.   Instantly the lead dog

dropped in his tracks but his face still turned westward
and he whimpered softly. The other huskies, too, had
raised the scent and strained at the breast straps,
eager to be off for the kill. Thorne banged the leash
threateningly over their heads commanding them to
lie down.

Carefully Jim studied the distances ahead of him.
He could see dark blotches moving slowly near the
western horizon. A slight wind blew across the Barrens from the northeast. If he drew closer to the
herd, he would be sighted before coming on range.
A sharp command brought the dogs to their feet.
Silver Chief led them back over the trail they had just
made, bearing slightly toward the running deer. The
team traveled for over an hour and when at last they
halted, the caribou were south of them and a little to
the west. The wind now fanned Thorne's face. He
was in a position to advance.

He unlimbered his rifle from its lashings and stretched
out on the sledge. In a low voice he ordered Silver
Chief forward once more, heading this time straight for
the band. One or two of the dogs began to whimper
impatiently, but a quick word silenced them. About
six hundred yards from the caribou, the hunter knew
he was sighted. One of the deer standing apart from
the others as a lookout, raised his head and saw the
oncoming team. Instantly he gave the signal and the

whole herd was under way, moving sluggishly at first, but soon gathering impetus for the stampede. Gradually they gained speed and soon were pounding along at a gallop. But Thorne had won his objective. He urged the dogs on for another hundred yards and then shouted at the lead dog.

"Gee, Chief—gee—gee."

Instantly the dog swung to the right and without slackening his pace, raced along almost parallel with the charging caribou, edging in toward them as he advanced. Thorne gauged the distance carefully and suddenly swung from the sledge. He dug his heels into the snow and pulled back on the "gee" pole.

"Whoa-whoa-Boy."

The team stopped. The Mounty dropped to the snow and opened fire. Three shots whipped out in quick succession. Two caribou plowed into the snow. Again and again the officer fired and when at last the herd had begun to bear away from the hail of bullets, eleven carcasses lay stiff and still on the snow.

Jim took a picket from the sledge, jammed it into the snow, and made the dogs fast. Then with knife and ax he set about the job of cleaning the deer. At noon he loaded three of them on his sledge and drove into camp. After a quick lunch he put his own dogs into the harness behind the Chief, turned Baker's huskies back to him, and the two men started back to the scene of the kill. Together they finished the cleaning job and late in the afternoon returned to the camp.

The little community buzzed with activity as they drove in. Meade was rushing the building of the new cabins. The whine of saws and the thud of axes sounded across the stillness. Some of the men were straining at the huge timbers, lifting them into place, while others moved back and forth carrying household furnishings into the huts that were already finished. As he watched the scene, Thorne felt a great happiness in his heart. Hope had once more taken hold of these people now that the onrush of the plague had been stopped. The sun was a flaming bonfire behind the spruce grove as he unhitched his team and fed them.

When breakfast was over the next morning, Thorne announced his decision to stay in camp and help Meade with the job of moving the sick. At the Store he carefully explained to the trappers where he had last seen the caribou herd. Then Baker, with Wright, Lowe, and the Indian, Charlie, formed a hunting party. When he had seen them on their way, Thorne went to find Meade.

Silver Chief, left to his own devices, roamed about the camp, dividing his time between Thorne and a general investigation of the little village. At last, assured that the Mounty was not going to stray far without him, the big dog chose a sunny spot in front of their cabin and stretched out to sleep.

It was noon when Silver Chief awakened. He treated himself to a delicious yawn, rose, and with forepaws stiff, arched his back in a mighty stretch. Suddenly he sensed that he was not alone and he turned swiftly toward the cabin. There, squatting on his haunches, sat a small, fat puppy. The pup gazed at the big wolf dog happily with his shining shoe-button eyes.

The hair along Silver Chief's neck rose in a stiff brush as he stood absolutely motionless, watching the cub. The pup staggered awkwardly to his feet and with a yelp of friendliness plunged toward the older husky. Silver Chief drew back quickly, his fangs bared, and growled a warning. The pup, startled by the growl, stopped in his headlong rush and dropped to his haunches again, his head cocked to one side in puzzled speculation.

The Chief remained still for a moment and then he, too, sank slowly to his haunches. The big dog was not at all sure what to make of this strange little animal who confronted him in such a friendly fashion. The Chief had not seen a puppy since the days when he had lived with his mother and brothers, and while instinct told him that here was one of his kind, he was nervous and distrustful. But the little fellow, full of the reckless courage of youth, was not to be discouraged by Silver Chief's aloof manner.

After sitting still as long as it was possible for any puppy to remain motionless, he suddenly tossed his head, sounded a wicked little bark, and advanced once more on the big dog. Rather he tried to advance, but moving forward all in one action was so difficult for his short, unmanageable legs that he toppled headfirst into the snow. Discouraged not a whit by this, he picked himself up and came to within a foot of the Chief, who lay like a stone image, forepaws stretched out, ears erect. Silver Chief was perplexed. This wriggling bunch of fur was something new and he had no idea how best to cope with it. It was so small, so harmless, and so friendly that it completely disarmed the husky. At last for want of something better to do, Silver Chief barked.

The result was panic. Coming so unexpectedly and at such close quarters, it nearly frightened the pup out of his wits. He emitted a squeal of terror and with the same awkward movements as before tried to come to his feet and retreat, but the best he could manage was a sprawling, undignified rout. From the safety of twenty yards, the little one sat regarding Silver Chief in awe and wonder. Then, his courage returning afresh, he began running in wide circles around the other dog, yipping his defiance. Silver Chief continued to sit perfectly still, only swinging his head about slowly to keep the pup in view.

When the cub had exhausted this pleasure without further reproof, he charged toward Silver Chief again. This time the big dog rose up to a sitting position and, allowing the little one to come close, bent his great head lower and lower until their noses touched. This delighted the pup and he rolled over on his back nibbling at the lead dog's jaws. Silver Chief rose and walked sedately around his tormentor, stopping every few paces to sniff noses with him again. Then he lay down, satisfied that all was well, and let the puppy go to work on him.

Growling in terrible ferocity, the pup tugged at the heavy fur around the Chief's neck and gnawed tirelessly at the huge paws. When he became too boisterous, the big dog lifted one of those paws and brushed him to the snow as if he were a fly. The pup grew frantic in his efforts to be everywhere at once, and the more annoying he tried to be, the more Silver Chief seemed to enjoy it. At times he gazed off away from the pup as if pretending to be bored by such antics, but actually he was growing to like this new kind of play more each moment. It was a new sort of companionship, a new sort of playmate, for the Chief who had never known anything but the friendship of one man.

The puppy gave him no rest. Over the big dog's back he clambered to slide down the sleek sides and land with a thump in the snow. The big tail, moving in quick circles, fascinated him, too, and his futile efforts to capture it and hold it with his tiny teeth drove him to a frenzy. Finally, despairing of the tail, he crawled up onto Silver Chief's neck where he opened a nipping campaign on the ears. Silver Chief shook his head and down the cub tumbled between his paws.

This stopped him for only a moment, then he staggered up and was off to the cabin steps in pursuit of some imaginary foe. Silver Chief rose and followed him, picking a spot near the hut to lie down. Once again the pup returned to the attack, and this time, assured that their friendship was sealed, his liberties were taken with the utmost confidence. Not until he dropped off to sleep, sheltered by the big paws of the sledge dog, did he give up the idea that he could wrestle Silver Chief to the snow.

Baker walked home with Jim that noon. As they approached, Silver Chief made no move to bound to them in greeting as was his custom. The trapper grinned as he looked down at the sleeping charge between the dog's paws.

"Well, will you look at that? he said softly to Thorne who stood looking on as if unable to believe his

eyes. "It's Mickey. His mother was killed by a wolf
this fall and one of my dogs had taken him to raise.
But it looks to me as if she had lost her job now."

Thorne nodded and walked to the door of the cabin.
Just before he went in, he looked back. Silver Chief
was watching him closely, his soft eyes pleading for
understanding. "I know I should go with you," he
seemed to be saying to his master, "but you see how it
is. You understand, don't you?" And Jim did understand. Grinning at the pair of them, he went inside
to fix lunch.

So Mickey, the waif, became the adopted pal of
Silver Chief. In the little cub, stumbling around him,
heavy-footed and happy, Silver Chief found a new out-
let for the native sense of protectiveness that was his
strongest heritage. As for Mickey, his feeling of
security grew each day. The combination was an
entirely satisfactory one for each of them.

Occasionally, however, the big dog grew impatient
of the constant tussling. Indeed, if he had possessed
man's power to analyze his feelings, he might at these
moments have questioned his wisdom in taking the
little one under his care. For Mickey, having been
once permitted liberties, took shameless advantage of
them. This was especially the case when the big
dog sought seclusion, so that he could stretch out to
doze in the warm sunshine. Greatly to the Chief's

discomfiture, Mickey refused to let him alone for any such delicious half hours.

The puppy, having decided that Silver Chief was his particular property, demanded attention at all times. Even at night, the hours when Silver Chief had made it his habit to lie peacefully beside his master, the cub persisted in being the center of attention, much to Silver Chief's annoyance and Thorne's amusement. A new order of things had come into being.

Lying in the corner while Jim prepared the evening meal, Silver Chief was forced to submit to the tireless charge of the little pup who never seemed convinced that he was incapable of getting the larger dog down. The tugging and nipping and tail chasing would continue for hours at a time while Silver Chief, with admirable patience, moved his head slowly from side to side to avoid the more frantic rushes. Occasionally he looked at Thorne as if to say, "Please don't think I've lost my good dog sense. Why, with one sweep of my paw I could put an end to all this. But what's a fellow to do?"

There were times when Silver Chief's patience did border on the breaking point, although these occasions were rare. They happened usually when the sharp little fangs cut through the skin of his ears. Then with a quick movement, he would paw Mickey to the floor with his big foot and hold him there for a moment while

the pup squealed in terror. Released, Mickey would
scramble away until he regained his bearings and then
return to strut with dignity around his friend while he
weighed the advisability of risking his neck under that
great paw another time. But soon he forgot his rebuff
and was at the Chief again.

Winship was deeply interested in the friendship
between the two dogs and spent a great deal of time
watching them and discussing the unusual combination
with Thorne. The manager believed the old theory
that dogs do have a power comparable to that of
humans for reasoning things out, that they do think.
Thorne could not agree. It was his idea, based upon
years of observation, that what was mistaken for
reason in a dog was simply instinct and a native trait
of taking the line of least resistance.

One night as the two men were having supper together in Jim's cabin, all manner of squeals and bumps
issued from beneath the bunk. In a moment out came
Mickey, proudly carrying one of the Mounty's moccasins. Holding his head high so that the soft boot
would not trip him, Mickey pranced to the center of
the floor, flopped down, and began to chew at the boot
vigorously. Thorne smacked the table sharply with
his hand.

"Drop that, Mickey. Drop it, I say. Drop that
moccasin."

Mickey looked at him, sniffed disdainfully, and went on with his work of destruction. Thorne rose and took a newspaper from the cupboard. He folded it quickly into a flat, ruler-like shape, and stepping over to the pup, smacked him smartly across his fat hind quarters. The blow fell with a loud slap and the effect was instantaneous. Mickey's bravery vanished quickly and with a howl he raced for Silver Chief, who had risen to his haunches at the first sound of Thorne's command to the pup. From his point of safety between the lead dog's legs, Mickey peered out at his master, his eyes blinking in hurt amazement. The Mounty returned to his meal.

"Did that hurt him much?" Winship asked.

Thorne grinned and shook his head. "Not a bit," he said. "I wouldn't hit him hard enough to hurt. That was just a little effort to curb the young man's fancy."

Dan looked at the whimpering pup, and Jim, noting the dubious expression on his friend's face, anticipated the question that he knew was coming. "You're thinking that maybe I'm a little rough on him, eh? Well, don't worry, Dan. The pup can take a lot worse than that without feeling any real pain. It's his pride that's hurting him now. That, and a bit of a dent in his self-confidence. The surest way to break a dog's spirit and turn him into a groveling, sneaking coward is to hurt him while he's young. Not only is it cruel

5

but it smashes all the faith he has placed in the man who is his master, and once that's gone, you can't restore it.

"It's like a bunch of kids on a football team. If they have a good coach, they place all their faith in him and play as he directs. Then they are beaten, and for awhile that faith is shaken. If they're beaten again and again, the faith crumbles and disappears for good. This is a case in point. That blow didn't hurt but the sound of it frightened him. And the fright wasn't as bad as the shock of receiving it from me. He's been looking to me for food, protection, and petting. Then I strike him and make a lot of noise doing it. That's what hurts. But mark my word, the little devil will be back stronger than ever in a little while. Right now he's telling his troubles to Silver Chief and I'll bet, if we could listen in, that wise old bird is pretending to sympathize, but deep down in his heart he knows that Mickey had it coming."

It was true. Long after the dishes were finished and the men sat talking, Mickey continued to crouch close to the protective strength of Silver Chief. Once in awhile he whimpered a little, and the big dog's tongue would flick out in an answering caress as if seeking to ease the pain in his little friend's heart.

"It does seem as if they were talking it over, at that," Winship remarked as he watched them.

Thorne nodded. "The pup will come around before long."

Before the lights were out that night, Jim took the cub in his arms and petted him for a long time, while Silver Chief pressed against his master's knee and looked on with approval. By the next morning all was forgotten.

IV

UNDER SUSPICION

WINSHIP'S theory that dogs could think was put to the test about a week later. He was helping Jim sew together some skin lashings. The dogs had been turned out for their morning romp when suddenly the men heard a piteous squeal followed by a short, warning bark from Silver Chief. Both men rushed to the door. Mickey lay trembling on the snow and beside him stood the Chief whimpering anxiously. At the sound of the opening door he turned toward his master. Jim saw the butt end of the ax under the pup's head and knew at once what had happened.

"Quick, Dan, pour some water from the kettle into a saucepan," Jim ordered as he hurried to the frightened

dog. Picking both Mickey and the ax up in his arms, he carried them into the cabin. Winship had the hot water ready in a basin. Gently Jim held the little dog's head down toward the water, letting the ax become slowly submerged. As the heat entered the steel, the pup's tongue which was stretched out on it like a red ribbon, suddenly came free. The cub looked up gratefully, moistened his chops once or twice, and then jumped down to the floor and raced to Silver Chief. The dog nosed him over in a quick inspection and then allowed him to hang on the ruff of his neck.

"There was meat on the ax," Thorne explained, "a few flakes of caribou left there from the chopping last night. Mister Inquisitive tried to lick them off and his tongue stuck."

Winship filled his pipe and resumed his sewing. After a moment, he asked, "Why did he lie still, Jim? He must have known you would come to his aid."

"I'm not so sure about that," the Mounty replied. "I figure it was instinct directing him to avoid pain. That squeal we heard was evidently the result of his trying to draw his tongue away from the steel. Flesh on steel doesn't hurt. It's trying to get away from the steel that is painful. There's also 'dog sense' to be considered when we try to analyze animals. For example, let a dog alone when he's hurt, and he'll cure himself quicker than we can. I remember I had a sledge dog once that broke his leg. I fixed him up in a splint but I didn't have to tie him down, for the simple reason that no power on earth could have made that fellow move until he was sure his leg was better."

"But what would have happened if we hadn't been here?" the manager persisted.

"Then I am afraid that Mickey would be without a tongue," was the answer. "And again it would be following the line of least resistance. Had he been alone, he would have lain till hunger or cold drove him to fight to get free. In that process, unless the steel had become warmed by the sun or by his body heat, he would have had a fine job getting the tongue loose. But once he saw that he could tear himself away, he would have preferred a few moments of pain to death by starvation."

And the talk continued on to various other examples of dog reasoning, the old controversy which will probably never be settled.

So time marched on through the winter months. Thorne had reported his activities by radio to Headquarters and had received orders to stay until the emergency was over. Although he realized that the emergency no longer existed, he was reluctant to leave. First there was the long, hard trip out on the winter trail, more than twice as grueling as the journey in, for this time he must sledge all the way to Churchill. He wanted to give his team a complete rest and plenty of time to build up on good deer meat before striking for home.

Besides he was very happy and contented at the camp. Hunting and visiting with these people appealed to him far more than months of inactivity at some Detachment, so he took advantage of Headquarters' orders. Meade was delighted, for he still needed a great deal of help before he could consider his little community in first-class shape again. Thus Jim decided to stay, not guessing that with this decision, the setting was laid for new adventures which, before they had run their course, were destined to bring fresh laurels to the Mounty and nearly to cost the life of Silver Chief.

Meanwhile Mickey's tutoring continued day by day. Baker's dog who had befriended the pup after his own mother had met her death, appeared more than glad to relinquish her charge to the care of the Chief. And although the pup continued to believe that everything Silver Chief did was in the spirit of play, actually the small dog was being coached in the things that were to prove invaluable to him later in life.

Long years before, Silver Chief's mother, Dee, had taught him in play those things which he afterwards used as weapons of offense and defense, and now he passed these lessons on to Mickey. For hours they romped about in the snow, Silver Chief diving quickly for the grip of the upper leg or the soft flesh beneath the throat. If he secured the leg, then he threw his little charge flat on his back. In the throat hold, however, the technique was different. Then the object was to hold on tight and bear the opponent to the snow.

Again there were the ripping flank thrusts, taught by the big dog in the form of stabbing nips along the pup's shoulders or hind quarters, an attack that, once mastered, would be the one used against wolves or in the chase when caribou were to be brought to earth.

Mickey was an apt pupil. He never seemed to tire and from the beginning displayed that valuable asset, a "never-quit" spirit which greatly impressed Thorne whenever he stopped to watch their tumblings. Often, without meaning to be rough, Silver Chief's grip would close down too hard or his toss would drop the little one upon his back with a terrific thud. Mickey at such times would stagger to his feet and circle about the big dog, stiff-legged and stiff-haired, while the Chief crouched in the snow waiting for the cub to regain his breath and his temper. His anger under control, Mickey would wade in again and the mock battle would go on.

After a time Silver Chief saw that his pupil was ready for the next course of instruction, and for hours the

K.WIESE

TOGETHER THEY STALKED PTARMIGAN, FLUSHED RABBITS,
INVESTIGATED THE SCENT OF CARIBOU.

two of them wandered away from the camp across the bleak, barren wastes or deep into the timber growths. Here again Dee's lessons were passed on, and the art of the hunt, the secrets of the game trails, became a part of Mickey's new wisdom. Together they stalked ptarmigan, flushed rabbits, investigated the scent of the caribou. Silver Chief was thorough in his training and would countenance no blundering. When the pup sought to rush headlong after the game, he was soundly thumped.

Once they came across a fresh trail of caribou. With a staggering bound Mickey was off, barking and yelping, threshing blindly through the snow. He was not sure what he was after but he knew that it was the scent of some animal. Silver Chief raced after him and pulled him down, holding him for some moments with his paw. Afterwards when the pup had quieted, they carefully circled the herd until the wind, heavily laden with the meat scent, fanned their noses. When Silver Chief succeeded in bringing down one of the laggards, Mickey's joy knew no bounds as they tore the hot meat from the carcass. Later on, when other deer were scented, Silver Chief kept the cub under close watch, showing him how to approach the herd up-wind, thus withholding their own scent from the deer until they were close enough to make a kill. All these things occupied days and weeks of patient hunting, but the little dog learned rapidly and all were lessons of great importance.

The winter was moving along. Each morning dawned with its long cracks of flaming color, the sky flushing brighter and brighter to give the North its short span of day, and then fading before the frosty points of the stars and the dazzling brilliance of the Northern Lights. December came. And Christmas. Christmas was a day of thanksgiving at Lake Caribou, spent quietly in the homes without celebration, only happy prayers because the Black Plague had been stamped out.

On one bleak, raw day in January the Doctor and Thorne prepared to install the last family in their new home. It was the Baker cabin, completed at last. Meade stayed in the new house, setting the last of the furnishings in order and keeping the fire blazing. At the old cabin Mrs. Baker put a hot-water bottle in the blankets, and then wrapping little Mildred snugly in their folds, handed her to Thorne. Together they walked across the slope and up the hill, Jim carrying the child gently while the mother walked by his side, keeping the blankets securely tucked around her daughter.

When he placed Mildred in her new bed, Jim made her a promise. "Sometime this week when you're stronger, I'm going to bring some visitors to see you."

Mildred's eyes danced and her thin little hands reached out to the Mounty. "Who, Sergeant Jim?" she pleaded. "Please tell me who."

Thorne shook his head and said in a serious tone, "Well, I don't know whether I should tell you or not." He turned to Meade who was standing by the kitchen stove. "Is she a pretty good girl about taking her medicine, Doctor?"

"You bet she is," Meade called back. "She's the best patient I ever had."

"In that event, Mildred, I'll have to tell you," the Mounty continued. "It's my dog, Silver Chief, and his little pal, Mickey. The Chief will take good care of you and see that Mickey, who's a bit of a roughneck, doesn't maul you. And when you're better, the Chief will take you for a long ride on the sledge. How would you like that?"

"O Mr. Thorne!" Mildred's small face lighted with a happy smile. "Please send them soon. I promise to get well as soon as I can, and I know that having them here will help."

"Won't you stay for some tea, Sergeant?" Mrs. Baker asked the Officer.

"No, thanks," Jim answered as he drew on his mitts. "I've got to get back early."

As he walked through the kitchen, Meade spoke to him. "Now that you mention them, I haven't seen

those dogs of yours today, Jim.   Don't suppose they've
run off, do you?''

"Not a chance, Doc.   They're just out tearing
around the country.   They'll show up at feeding time.
See you at the Store tonight, Doc."

Back at his own quarters, Thorne busied himself
making out the weekly log which he had kept since his
arrival.   As the sun swung low in the west, he went
outside, chopped up some deer meat, and fed the dogs.
Silver Chief and Mickey had not yet put in their
appearance, but he did not worry about them.   He
remembered times a year or two back when the big
wolf dog, feeling the call of the wild, had left to roam
the timber for days at a stretch.   But as the Chief had
become accustomed to camp life, his desire to roam had
disappeared, and now Jim felt sure that the two dogs
had only strayed far afield in their play.

He re-entered the cabin and prepared his supper.
As he was ready to take it from the stove, there came
a scratch on the door.   When Jim opened it, Silver
Chief glided into the room like a gray shadow, coming
quickly to Jim's knee for his customary pat of welcome.

"You're late, Old Timer.   Where have you been?
And where's Mickey?"   As he talked, Jim shredded the
husky's meat into a pan and put it down on the floor.
Mickey, Jim decided, must have found one of the sledge
dogs neglecting his supper and seized the opportunity

to help himself to a choice piece of meat. It was a habit of Mickey's, and Thorne thought no more about it. Silver Chief finished eating and stretched out in the corner, licking his chops. After a second cup of coffee, the Mounty called for his parka and mitts.

"Let's go down and see what the town gossip is, Chief," he said as the dog brought his clothes. Together they went out the door and down the trail to the Store.

As he entered the Store, Jim wondered a little at seeing so many of the trappers around the Post at night. Doubtless the siege of illness had prevented the men from extending their lines for any greater distance than could be worked by a swing-around trip of a day or two. Baker, Lowe, and Wright were bending over the counter, apparently examining something of great interest. Winship stood behind them, a worried look on his ruddy face. As the Mounty came up to them, the men all turned to look at him, and conversation came to a standstill.

Silver Chief, instead of trotting to his usual corner, advanced slowly toward the silent men. Jim noticed with amazement that the hair along the dog's neck was standing upright.

Thorne was the first to speak. "What's going on?" he asked. "You look as if you were hatching a deep plot of some sort."

Lowe and Parker drew back and Thorne saw that Wright was holding Mickey. The pup's eyes sought Thorne's and he whined pleadingly. Silver Chief, still standing by his master, growled. Jim looked questioningly from one man to another, and was about to speak when Meade, who had bent down behind the counter to get some tobacco, straightened up.

"Glad you came in, Jim," he said gravely. "Take a look at that pup's paws and mouth."

Thorne stared at the Doctor as if unable to understand his meaning. Then he stepped up to the counter and picked up one of the small paws. There were tufts of golden fur between the toes. He examined the little mouth. There was dried blood along the lips, and minute scraps of reddish meat still clung to Mickey's whiskers.

"Well, what's it all about?" Jim demanded.

"Just this, Sergeant." It was Lowe who answered. "We've been losing a lot of fox the last few weeks, and this gives us a pretty good idea where they've gone."

Jim burst out laughing. "You're not trying to tell me that you think Mickey has been robbing your traps. Why, the little sucker couldn't lift a trap, much less pull a carcass out of one."

Meade had packed his pipe and was holding a match to it. When it was drawing freely, he began to speak. "No, we're not fools enough to think anything like that, Jim," he said. "But we do know that Silver Chief is big enough to rob a trap. He and the cub have been away from the camp a lot in the past few weeks. In fact those losses started just about the time the two of them began wandering off."

Thorne's smile vanished as he looked down at Silver Chief still standing at his side. Without a word the Officer dropped to his knees. He took the dog's great head between his hands and turned it slowly first to one side and then to the other so that he could see the underside of the jaws. The men leaned down to watch his inspection. There was not a sign of incriminating evidence. Next Thorne examined the dog's paws. Every man in the group could see that there was not the slightest trace of blood or meat or fur on the lead dog. Thorne drew a breath of relief and rose to his feet. He fished for a cigarette and lighted it before he spoke.

"I think you boys are a bit hasty in your deductions. In the first place you can see for yourselves that the Chief shows no evidence of having been near your traps. And secondly, you know as well as I do that a dog hates the flesh of fox and eats it only when he's starving. I don't have to tell you how rank and strong it is."

Lowe spoke up and it was plain that he was still convinced of the dog's guilt. "We know that, Thorne.

6

But we know too that a wolf ain't so fussy.   And the Chief has got plenty of wolf in him."

With those words he dropped the little dog to the floor and stood back, looking at Jim with an air of finality. Mickey ran to Silver Chief, who led him off to their corner.   The pup began to tussle happily with the big dog, oblivious of the fact that he was the center of this bitter discussion.

Lowe had scored a point and Thorne realized it. It was true that Silver Chief had wolf blood in him, and it was true too that a wolf would kill and eat a fox every chance he had.   But Silver Chief?   Thorne looked at him, lying in his corner playing with the little dog.   Why, Silver Chief wouldn't do a thing like this. He would never touch anything that was man's. Yet the blood on Mickey was surely fox blood.   Where had he got it?

"Ever hear of a wolverine?" the Mounty asked suddenly.

Baker nodded.   "Sure, a wolverine is a robber. I've had them follow me around just waiting for me to make a catch and when I did, they'd tear it out of the trap and sit there laughing at me.   But there haven't been any around here for years.   Anyhow, that doesn't account for the stuff on the pup's paws and chops."

Thorne realized that the men had a real grievance. Trapping was their livelihood.   Protection against theft was their right, and he, as an officer of the law, was sworn to uphold that right. Now the safety of their bread and butter was endangered and they were justified in demanding a showdown, even though he himself was their friend and the cause of their losses was his dog.

"Look here, boys," Jim spoke earnestly, "this is a tough spot for me. You all know how I feel about that dog. You all have that same sort of feeling yourself. And I want you to know that I won't spare him or myself if you can prove your case. But why aren't there any signs on Silver Chief, too? As yet you haven't proved a thing against him."

"Take it easy, Jim," the Doctor said. "We all know how much you love that dog, and he is a beauty, and we haven't forgotten the job he did bringing in the serum. You can be sure we don't want to be unfair. But you realize what robbing traps means to us up here. If it was a man and you caught him, it would mean a jail sentence, a stiff one. If it's the dog—well, you know what has to be done."

"Yes." Jim's face was grave as he looked toward his dog. "If the Chief has been doing this, he'll have to be shot." He turned back to the men. "But he hates traps. And what on earth would he do with the frozen carcass?"

"They must have come across a freshly trapped one," was Meade's guess. "That's the reason for the blood on Mickey.   Chief is older and wiser.   He could clean away all the signs.   Besides there are lots of cases on record where wolves robbed traps and hid the animals.   It seems as if they steal just because they get a kick out of it."

Thorne dropped his cigarette and trod on it.   Pulling on his mitts, he started for the door.   The two dogs were at his heels instantly.   At the door he turned back.

"Let me have a little time to work this thing out, boys.   I'm not convinced yet that you're right, but if you are, I'll take the necessary steps."   Then he went out into the darkness.   He had gone scarcely a hundred feet when Baker, who had followed him out, hailed him.   Baker walked along silently beside him for a moment.   Then he spoke.

"What do you figure on doing, Sergeant?"

"I'm going to make an investigation of those trap lines first," Jim said.

"You'll use Silver Chief, I suppose," Baker inquired.

"Yes, I'll need him in the team, and besides if he is in on this business, he may get panicky and lead me to his cache."

"I'm sorry, Thorne."   Baker stopped and held out his hand.   "The fellows are pretty sore, but I hope you can prove us wrong.   You'd better leave Mickey with me while you're gone.   He'll be company for Mildred, and I'll see that nothing happens to him."

"Thanks, Baker. I'll do that. Good night."
Baker turned back and Jim went on home.

In his own cabin, Jim stoked up the fire and made
ready for bed. Placing the lamp on the table, he sat
down before the stove to have a last smoke and to
think things over. Silver Chief came to his side and
laid his smooth head on Thorne's knee, waiting for the
hand he loved to stroke the softness of his ears and
jaws. Mickey danced about for a few minutes in an
attempt to break up this nightly ritual between dog
and master, but when he saw that his efforts were of
no avail, he tumbled off to his corner and was soon
asleep.

But tonight Thorne did not feel the contentment
that this quiet period of the evening had always meant
to him before. Silver Chief a thief! His dog a robber
of traps! The evidence was strong but Jim could not
bring himself to believe the accusation. The dog was
too fine for that, too fair. Why, he was as fair as any
man. He had been fair in his resentment when Jim
had captured him. There had been nothing sneaking
or sly in his fight against Thorne's persuasiveness. He
was a brave, savage fighter who had given up the life
of the wilds only after a long struggle, and then for a
better life and a greater love. He was fair in his
dealings with other dogs. The word "bully" could
never be used about the Chief. He was more than

fair in return to Jim for his kindness. Where there was work to be done or privation to be endured, he did his part with the same spirit of good sportsmanship that Thorne hoped he himself would show under those conditions. And they had called him a thief.

Thorne knew that he had schooled the dog well. Clothing, harness, food, traps, everything that was man's—by long, patient instruction Jim had impressed on the dog that these were not to be touched. Besides there was the dog's native distrust, his instinct to avoid anything in the wilds that had the scent of man. More than once the Mounty had seen his dog circle an area that held traps, an area contaminated by the dangerous odor of man.

Yet the men of the camp had made their accusation, and he was faced with the duty of disproving their evidence or destroying the guilty one. As he thought of the latter, his grip tightened on the silky ear and Silver Chief looked up at him, trying to show in his soft eyes that he returned this sudden gesture of love his master had shown him. Destroy the dog! Surely they would not demand that. Surely he could take him away. These trappers were his friends. They would understand. They knew how he loved the dog, and if he took him away to the South and kept him at Headquarters Detachment, their demand for justice would be satisfied.

But in his heart the Officer knew this was wrong. Only too well his conscience told him that he was seeking to protect his pet and to avoid the rigid code of duty. If a man robs a bank in one place, he is not taken to another and allowed to start again, to rob other banks. He must pay for his crime.

Thorne bent low and held the splendid head close to his face. Deep in Silver Chief's chest a rumble sounded, a love growl, and the dog pressed closer to the man. Jim smoothed the sleek sides and gently stroked the head and chest.

"We'll see, Old Timer. We'll give them a run for their money. Nobody will ever persuade me that you're a criminal."

V

HITTING THE TRAIL

THE next morning when Silver Chief came to rouse his master, he found him already awake. Jim reached out for the big dog and gave him an unexpected and pleasant tussle. Delighted with this unusual procedure, the Chief backed away from him and started to lope, side prance, around the room. Mickey stumbled joyfully after him, wanting his share in this before-breakfast romp.

Thorne lay smoking a cigarette and watching the two dogs thoughtfully. At last he rose, lighted the fire, and turned the huskies out of doors. Next he hurried into his clothes and prepared breakfast. This was to be a busy day. He was going to hit the trail, armed with determination to disprove the trappers' charges.

Jim could not guess who was robbing the traps, how they did it, or for what reason. But he was convinced that Silver Chief was innocent and he meant to back up his faith in the dog with every possible effort.

While breakfast cooked, Jim went to the picket line. His slap of greeting to each dog was a warning that they were in for a run that day. He slid the big sledge down in front of the cabin where sleeping bag, trail stove, coal oil, a big chunk of caribou, and his grub box were loaded and lashed. Rifle and ax were secured and the harness shaken out and stretched along in front. Then he went inside to eat, being careful to bring the Chief and Mickey in with him. He was taking no chances with the touchy temper of some trapper who might decide to take matters into his own hands with a rifle.

Jim had not finished his breakfast when the door of the cabin opened on Baker, Lowe, and Indian Charlie. Silver Chief rose with a growl while Mickey scrambled to safety between his legs. Jim silenced the lead dog with a look. It was the presence of the Indian that had caused Silver Chief's unfriendliness. He had grown accustomed to white men and seldom resented them, but he had never lost his hate of the Indians.

Jim greeted his callers cordially. "Drag up a chair, boys, and have some coffee. There's plenty in the pot."

The three men refused uneasily. There was a tension about them as if they wanted to get what they had to say over with as quickly as possible. Thorne studied them with interest.

He liked Baker, had warmed to him from the first. As the big trapper slouched down onto the bunk, fumbling for his pipe, Jim could not help feeling that here was a man whose kindliness and sympathy would make him insist on fair play under any conditions.

Lowe was an entirely different type, lean and hard, a bachelor. Here was a man who had lived alone in a stern country so long that every sensibility in him had turned hard and embittered. As Jim looked at the thin face, the cold, agate eyes, he knew that Lowe would be exacting and unreasonable.

As for the Indian, some one of his race, like that of the white man, was now and then found to be untrustworthy, and this one seemed inclined in that direction. He was squat, tattered, and surly. On his flat, copper-colored face with its brilliant black eyes, were all the signs of a sly, selfish nature. At the moment his lips were parted in a disagreeable smile which showed his pleasure in having some part in a situation that meant trouble for the Mounty. As Lowe came forward, Indian Charlie shuffled along beside him. The Indian carried a dirty bundle wrapped in burlap. Lowe took it from him and unrolled it on the table. It was the torn and blood-crusted carcass of a small, white fox.

The trapper looked straight at Thorne. "Here's more evidence for you, in case you haven't enough already." Lowe did not try to hide the sneer in his voice. He turned to the Indian. "Tell him where you found this," he ordered.

The Indian's eyes could not stand the direct gaze of the officer and he kept looking from the dead fox to Jim and back again. Fumbling with a rag of the animal's torn skin, he began to speak.

"My line three miles south from here. It run south to Swift River. Halfway there is trap, and this morning I come to trap and see tracks all around. They not wolf tracks or wolverine. They dog tracks and they lead away into bush where is much snow turned up like something has been dragged. I look at trap close and find front paw of white fox still there. Then I follow tracks and come to log half mile away. Beside log is this." Here the Indian jabbed at the carcass. "It buried in deep drift. Your dog do this. I want to shoot your dog." The Indian shook his gun and Lowe advanced menacingly toward Silver Chief.

With an oath Thorne leaped to his feet. His lips set in a hard, straight line and his words crackled as he spoke.

"One more remark like that and I'll throw you both out of here. Remember I'm the law in this country, and if you can't present your case in a respectful manner, I'll teach you some manners. Understand this. Owning the dog that you think is guilty of robbing your traps doesn't change my position in the slightest. I represent His Majesty's Government and as long as I do, I'll run this show in my own way. Now go on over there, both of you, and sit down."

Indian Charlie, frightened by the outburst, started hastily toward the bunk but Lowe continued to stare insolently at the officer. Their eyes held each other until at last the trapper gave way and went to sit down on the bunk. But he was not cowed by the vehemence of Thorne's words. Lowe's courage was the kind that increased under fire. Harsh and unfair though he might be, there was no yellow streak in his make-up.

The Indian was plainly uneasy, and Silver Chief's constant growls did not help to make him easier. The faint, distinctive odor of smoked meat and skins that is always in the air when an Indian is about was stimulating the dog's desire to leap at the man. Jim knew that all huskies hated Indians, but this dog seemed to hate them more than most. Jim had often wondered about it, but there would have been no mystery had he known of that frosty morning so many years before when Silver Chief had suddenly seen his mother topple over dead beside him. That morning Silver Chief had known the Indian scent for the first time, and he had never forgotten that the first sorrow of his life had been caused by a Red Man.

Thorne lighted a cigarette, wanting to regain his self-control before he carried on the investigation. He must view this thing from his position as an officer of the law. And that was difficult to do when Silver Chief was involved. But he must set his own feelings aside.

He turned to Baker. "How many men are trapping out of this Post?"

Baker thought for a moment. "Six," he answered. "There's Howell and Lewis and Wright, that's three. Then Lowe, myself, and Indian Charlie. No, seven. There's Charlie's brother. He'll be out in another week."

Thorne pondered this information for a while and his gaze went back to the fox on the table.

"This is a white," he said. "That means there's a run on."

Baker nodded. "They've been coming down heavy for two weeks. You remember, Jim, you figured they would that time you went out and found the caribou herd. First run we've had in years."

"And we've got to sit here arguing about it while that blasted dog of yours takes money right out of our pockets," Lowe broke in hotly. "Quit your talking, Thorne, and turn that dog over to us."

"That's about enough from you, Lowe," Jim answered quietly. "Perhaps you didn't hear me a moment ago when I said I was handling this thing without any suggestions from you. I don't need to tell you that I'm the law in this part of the country."

The trapper glared at the Mounty but said nothing. Jim smoked in silence. So there was a run, the dream of every trapper. Then the land swarms with fox and the men are hard-pressed to keep the carcasses removed from the traps so that more can be taken. Small fortunes are made when a run is on, and Jim realized that with fur selling from twelve to twenty-two dollars a pelt the losses would amount to thousands if they were allowed to continue.

"Any idea how many pelts you've lost so far?" he demanded of Baker.

"Yes, sir. Got the list right here." Baker pulled a soiled slip of paper from the pocket of his shirt. Tilting the paper to the light he read, "Lowe, twelve. Howell, nine. Myself and Lewis, seven each. And Charlie, two. That's thirty-seven all told. We figure it at about four hundred dollars."

Thorne made a note of the information, setting the men's names alongside the number of skins each had lost.

He turned to Baker. "Can you be ready to go on the trail with me this morning?" he asked.

Baker nodded. Jim walked to the stove and poured himself another cup of coffee. As he stirred in the sugar, he spoke to the men once more. "Here's what I'm going to do. I want to see the signs of this stealing you're talking about, myself. Baker and I will make a swing around the circuit and check up. And I'm taking Silver Chief. If he's with me, and the trap losses continue, then it's pretty sure proof that you're wrong. If I find his marks along the line and if there are no more losses while we're gone——" Jim hesitated, then went on. "Well, I'll handle the dog the way I'd pass judgment on any other. That's all. Baker, I'll be ready in about half an hour."

The men rose and went out the door. It had barely closed when Jim noticed that Charlie had forgotten the evidence. He stepped to the door and called him. "Hey, you, Charlie."

The Indian came slowly back. "Take that thing out of here." Jim pointed to the carcass on the table. Charlie picked up the stiff body and wrapped it in the piece of burlap sack. On the table lay a pair of short, embroidered mitts, the kind used to handle traps, always carried on the sledge away from the food or clothing so that the odor of food or gear does not come in contact with them. Jim picked them up, admiring the beaded pattern absently as he continued to think about the Chief. "Here, you'll forget these next," he said and handed them to the Indian.

Thorne began immediate preparations for the trail. He pulled on a heavy pair of moose-hide, ankle-high moccasins, and set aside two extra pairs to be placed in the spare clothes bag. With his uniform breeches he wore a heavy-duty shirt. Mitts and parka and his service revolver, together with plenty of ammunition, completed the outfit.

Silver Chief saw that they were going on a trip and came to his master eagerly. Jim could never understand why the huskies loved to be in harness. The work was grueling; it meant cut and bleeding feet, and often they must go for days with scarcely any food. Yet as long as they could stand, the dogs would plead to go forward. The big lead dog was even more anxious to be in harness than the average husky, and this despite the fact that he invariably pulled twice as much as the rest of them. When the rest of them were hanging in their traces, the Chief was always slogging along tirelessly.

Jim, carrying his clothes bag and his gun, went outside with the dogs. He strapped the Chief carefully into his place at the lead. This was a great moment for Mickey, who pranced about gripping both the traces and Silver Chief's neck with equal vigor. The other dogs were led down from the picket line. Jim allowed each of them to walk close to Silver Chief while a sort of sniffing greeting took place. When the inspection had proved satisfactory both to the leader and to the other dog, he was harnessed into place. Soon they were all lying on the snow, whining their eagerness to be off.

Thorne picked up Mickey and much to the youngster's surprise, slung him on top of the load. A quick turn of the lash end across his back held him secure. While the pup wailed his terror from his high perch, the officer shouted to Silver Chief and the team moved off swiftly. Straight for the Store they raced. Here Jim brought them to a halt and went inside with the pup to await Baker and talk to the Doctor.

Meade greeted him warmly. He had heard about the talk in the cabin, and he had no doubt of the Mounty's intention to handle the situation fairly.

"Need anything in the way of supplies, Jim?" Winship called from behind the counter.

"Thanks, no, Dan. I'm all set, I think." Jim handed the pup to Doctor Meade. "I want you to take this chap to Mildred Baker, Doc. I promised her she could have both dogs for a visit, but I'll be using the Chief for a few days. Besides, the pup will be safe there. No telling what some of these hot-heads might do. You'll see that he gets a run each day, won't you?"

Meade nodded and rumpled Mickey's furry head. The cub accepted the challenge and went to work on the Doctor's thumb.

"How long do you figure on being gone?" Meade asked.

"Till I get this thing cleared up. It shouldn't take more than a week."

"Well, I'm rooting for you, Son. You know that. So is everyone else, for that matter, but you can understand how they feel. We've had two tough seasons, and what with the sickness and all, things are in pretty bad shape. But I have a hunch that they're wrong about the Chief. By George, I hope so. That's a dog for a man, you've got there. And don't worry about this fellow." The Doctor grinned down at Mickey. "If he doesn't amputate my thumb before you leave, I'll deliver him to Mildred and keep an eye on him while you're gone. Here's Baker now."

The trapper stuck his head inside the door. "All set, Thorne?" he called.

Jim went outside to where the two teams were drawn up.

"How much caribou are you taking for dog feed?" Baker wanted to know.

"About a week's ration," was the reply. "If we stay longer or get held up by bad weather, we'll have to shoot food."

Baker nodded his agreement. "All right. Let's go. I'll lead off." He walked to his sledge and unloosed a long whip. Jim took his stand beside his load. The whip snapped over the dogs' heads and they came to their feet. The first team led off with a rush, heading southwest from the camp. Thorne allowed Baker about a quarter mile's start and then ordered Silver Chief to "mush." The big team eased against the breast straps, all moving at one time, and the long sledge swayed easily across the crusted snow.

It was good to get out on the trail again. The dogs, freshened by days of rest and good food, felt the zest of strength and freedom surge through their blood, and they made easy work of the sledge. Indeed they were so eager that Jim had to swing back constantly on the "gee" pole to hold his specified distance behind Baker. The day was cold and dazzling. A little way out the officer halted his team and took his dark glasses from the duffel bag. Snow blindness was a thing to be avoided, and the colored lenses softened the glaring whiteness which danced off the sparkling snow. When the glasses were adjusted and the bag re-lashed, he continued on his way.

The first three miles of the trail were used by the trappers and consequently were hard-packed. This made for easy going. Later on, Jim had an idea there would be a division of the trails as they came to the point where each trapper struck off on his own. Then it would be harder going. But for the moment he was forced to trot to keep the pace set him by the dogs. The country appeared to be almost flat, but actually they were moving along the side of a gentle slope which diminished slightly as they advanced. Traveling conditions were ideal, and ordinarily Thorne would have enjoyed being on the trail again, but today he could not shake the troubled feeling that gripped him every time he looked at Silver Chief.

Jim had no idea just how he was going to disprove the charges against the wolf-dog. The notion that a man might be responsible for the losses had occurred to him, but he had dismissed it as foolish. All these men had lived and worked together for years. Each had his own territory and was kept busy covering his own line. When fur was plentiful, they all made money, and when it was scarce, they all suffered. No, something else was at the bottom of this, and he had to admit that all the evidence pointed strongly toward his dog. Nevertheless he refused to accept the verdict and went on his way with a desperate hope that something would turn up to aid his defense of the Chief.

At noon Baker called a halt. Jim's team dropped down for a rest while he walked on ahead. The trapper pointed out the division of the trails, one swinging abruptly almost due west, the other bearing

BAKER POINTED TO THE WEST TRAIL.

off to the southeast. Ahead was a heavy stand of timber.

Baker pointed to the west trail. "That's where my line runs, Sergeant. Then from the end of it there are cross-over trails to the rest of the boys' lines. In fact they make a swing right around this ridge ahead of us and come out here." He pointed to the southeast trail. "This is Indian Charlie's and his brother's. Now where do you want to start?"

Jim considered the trails for a moment. Then he answered. "I figure the best bet is for us to go on together for a while. We'll start off along your line so you can pick up anything you might have taken, and you'll not lose too much time on this job with me. Then we'll work over to the others for a look around. If we see that it's going to take too long or that we might get held up, you can shove off for home and I'll just poke around on my own."

"Okay, Sergeant. Hey, Red." Baker's shouted command brought his team to their feet. "Hi—hi—hike. Gee. Gee." The huskies swung to the right and trotted off along Baker's trap line. Jim went back to his own team and was soon following the others.

After an hour's travel Baker stopped again. This time when Thorne walked up to the front sledge, Baker was busy unlashing his load. "Got a trap in here," he said. "I'm going to run in and see what's happened since I was out last." From his load he took a long, flat knife. Then he untied a pair of gloves which had been dangling from a string on the side of the load. These he substituted for the fur gauntlets he had been wearing. As Baker walked off the main trail, Jim sat down on the sledge and lighted a cigarette.

When Baker had gone about fifty yards, he came to a small, rocky outcrop on the side of a slope. Here he stopped and looked carefully around. Then, stepping carefully from stone to stone, he advanced until he came to a little clump of spruce. Again he stopped, and this time he shouted back to Jim.

"Nice silver here, Jim. Want to take a look?"

The Mounty rose and tossed away his smoke. Baker called out again. "Do you mind bringing that bait bag? It's on the front end there."

Thorne took a small canvas bag from the front of the sledge and went off down the trail, taking care to set his feet in the same tracks that Baker had made. When he reached the rocks he, too, used them as stepping stones. Jim, although he was not a trapper, knew enough about the work to realize that care must be taken in approaching and handling traps. No animal in the world is as quick as the fox to get the scent of man. That was why it was essential to eliminate all traces of odor.

When he reached Baker, the trapper was pointing to the base of a small tree where the snow was badly churned. A lovely silver fox lay rigid on the snow, one foot held fast in the steel jaws of the trap. The fox lay like a pool of shimmering oil against the white snow, the silky sheen of its coat dark at the base nearest the skin and lightening at the tips. As he looked at it, Jim was struck with its beauty and thought how horrible it was that anything so lovely had to die such a painful death. Such a glorious creature of God should live and be free rather than perish in this awful death of freezing and starvation as it lay helpless for hours, gripped in the merciless steel jaws. Then Jim pursed his lips a little at these thoughts. No matter how cruel it seemed, life must always be a battle between the strong and the weak, and the weak were destined to suffer.

Baker knelt down and pulled the trap jaws apart. He lifted the dead animal and gave it to Thorne. "I'll just reset this and then we'll be on our way," he said.

Thorne watched with interest as the trapper went about the business of setting the trap. The jaws were smooth, neither sharp nor edged, so there was little blood. They did not cut the leg but crushed it and held it firmly. Carefully Baker opened the jaws wide and held them in that position by the trap. The trap was attached to the tree by a chain to prevent it from being dragged away. Baker put the trap down about a foot from the base of the tree. Then using the flat edge of the big knife, he lifted little mounds of snow and dusted them over the trap and all around it until every evidence of disturbance was gone. Next he took the bait bag from Thorne. It contained pieces of spoiled seal meat which had been brought down from the North by canoe in the summer and allowed to decay, and its stench rose to the heavens. The fox likes bad meat and its scent carries for miles, luring him to the spot where the trap is hidden.

The bait was shredded in small pieces and sprinkled around the trap for about four feet. Some of it was covered and some of the more tempting morsels were left on the surface. Once the fox found these, he would paw beneath the snow for more until the trap snapped his foot for the fatal capture.

When the bait was distributed, the men carefully retraced their steps. Jim went first, using the same trail they had made as they came in. Baker followed and at every step he turned, stooped down, and with his knife dusted the snow across their footsteps. When they had returned to the sledge, all signs of their presence were completely covered.

Soon they were under way again, and before darkness threatened, they had picked up two more pelts, both whites.   At each trap they stopped, for Thorne wished to examine the snow around them.   Nor was his search in vain.   Twice he came across paw marks, and they were not those of a fox or a wolf.   They were the prints of a dog.   More than that, each time they came to a halt by a trap, Silver Chief stirred about uneasily.   Lying in the snow at the head of the team, he would turn restlessly toward the spot where Jim and Baker bent over the trap.   Once or twice he whined.

Jim saw all this, and so did the trapper.   Neither man commented on it but Jim felt a terrible sensation of fear inside him.   The dog's actions and the footprints were piling up evidence against him, and Jim knew that the trapper's belief in the husky's innocence was rapidly waning.

VI

A SHOT IN THE BACK

THORNE and the trapper camped that night on the hillside near a stand of timber. The dogs were picketed and supper started. Boughs were cut and set near the fire and the bed rolls spread out on them. Silver Chief as usual was left free but he made no attempt to leave the camp. Instead he ate his supper by the fire and then came to doze contentedly near Thorne. While the tea and beans were heating, the men changed into dry socks, hanging their wet ones to dry on small twigs before the fire.

After supper the two men smoked in silence. The sky was dark and overcast. In summer, it would have heralded rain, but the cold held on and they kept the fire piled high with wood. Across the hill a wolf howled and the dogs stirred uneasily at their chains. Silver Chief lifted his head and sniffed the air. For a long time he looked out into the darkness as if he yearned to answer that call and leap away across the snow to find his brothers. But at last he turned back to Jim. The Mounty stroked him gently and soon the dog rested his head once more on his outstretched paws.

Baker had been watching the lead dog without a word. At last he took his pipe from his mouth. "It would be a shame to lose him, Jim," he said.

Thorne nodded. "Baker, what's your opinion of this thing? How do you account for the loss of the fur?"

"Up until today I've been with you," was the answer. "Somehow I couldn't believe that the Chief would do it. But since this afternoon—well, you saw how he acted."

Both men were silent for a while. Then the trapper went to his clothes bag and pulled out a small notebook with a pencil attached to it. "I'm going to draw you a chart of the trapping layout in this district," he said. "I figure that after I've set you straight on the trails around here, you'll be able to find your way all right without me. Somehow I don't feel just right about being with you while you conduct this investigation."

The trapper looked straight at Jim as he said this, and then his eyes dropped to the page he was thumbing. Thorne saw at once what Baker meant and was grateful for his sympathy. Baker didn't want to be in on any discovery Jim might make which would condemn Silver Chief. If the Mounty were to find that the charges brought against his dog were true, it was his affair, and Baker wanted to leave him free to handle it in any way he saw fit. The trapper hadn't forgotten that it was Thorne who had saved his little girl's life, and this was his chance to prove his gratitude. Thorne's hand went out to Silver Chief's head. He realized deeply what a fine thing Baker was doing.

The trapper was busy with his drawing for some time. Occasionally he stopped to warm his hands at the fire. At moments he seemed uncertain and sat with the pencil at his lips, studying the lines he had made, while the firelight chased shadows across his rugged, brown face. At last he was finished and moving closer to Jim, he spread the chart out on his knees. The map resembled the lines on the palm of a hand, the trap lines fanning out from a base plainly marked Lake Caribou. Baker pointed to this name and began his explanation.

"That name is all wrong. There isn't any lake there as you know, only a widening out of the river.

The Indians gave it the name Lake Caribou years ago. Any marsh or widespread stream is a lake to them."

The man pointed to a heavy line. "Here's the trail we came out on. All of us use that trail. Then here," his pencil followed along the line that swung west from the main trail, "here's my line, the one we are on now. It runs in this direction about thirty-five miles. I've been able to work all my line but the rest of the boys have only been able to work a small part of theirs, what with being tied up with sickness and everything. Theirs are farther away, as you can see. Here's Lewis', south and more west than mine. Wright's and Howell's run farther south, with Howell's swinging east after it crosses Swift River. That's all in this district. Over on the other side," here the pencil moved east, "are Lowe's and Indian Charlie's and his brother's. They run pretty parallel. The Indian's is much longer than Lowe's or any of the rest of them. The two of them, he and his brother, cover over two hundred miles. That's why they have a shack at the far end. They sledge in a little grub early in the winter and then as they make their swing around, they can hole up and re-outfit any time they want."

"These lines are pretty sharply divided, aren't they?" the officer commented. "You and one bunch away over here to the west, and the others in the east. What's the idea of that?"

"A height of land runs directly between us, that, and pretty heavy timber. It's no mountain or anything like that, but just high enough to give the fox a good lookout when they cross over. Then they den along the edges of the slopes on this side and the other side where there are lots of rocks and a little timber."

Thorne took the map and studied it for a few minutes while Baker re-lighted his pipe. "I don't see any reason why you should make this whole trip with me," the Mounty said finally. "This chart is very clear. Suppose you come along with me until we reach Swift River, then double-back and take care of your traps. Time away from them means money to you. I'll hit off down the river and work back along Lowe's line. Then I'll come back into camp for a day or two to rest the dogs and get some supplies. There will be time enough after that to go over Charlie's line. How far down the river will I have to travel before striking these other lines?"

"About fifty miles. You can't miss the place to turn in for Lowe's. There's a long point jutting out into the stream and a big, bare rock that sets back about fifty feet from the river's edge on the north side. If you don't need me, I would like to keep busy. When there's a run, I don't want to miss my share." Baker stood up and stretched. "Right now, I'm turning in."

THE POWERFUL JERK SPUN HIM ABOUT SO QUICKLY THAT HE
DROPPED TO THE SNOW.

Later as the fire smoldered low and darkness crept nearer, Baker's voice came from deep within the folds of his sleeping bag. "Funny about a dog, isn't it, Sergeant? I mean the way you get attached to them. What do you suppose is the reason? I know lots of men I call my friends, and yet I've owned dogs that were closer to me than any man has ever been. You're the same way about the Chief, I guess."

"I don't know what it is that makes you feel that way about a dog," the Mounty replied. "Maybe it's his loyalty. Whatever goes wrong, a dog will always stick and seems to understand. That might be the reason. But there's something more to it than that, and I don't know what it is."

The big, gray dog that lay beside him moved closer at the sound of his master's voice. Jim could feel his warmth through the sleeping bag. Soon he heard the dog sigh deeply, satisfied that everything was well with this man for whose welfare he felt so responsible. Jim stared into the darkness for a long time, watching the clouds part before the pale glory of the moon. The embers cracked a little and dropped. At last the woods became a place of long, deep shadows as the men and the dogs slept in the cold silence.

It must have been nearly three when the camp was thrown suddenly into an uproar. The savage barking of the dogs woke Thorne with a start, and as he

8

struggled up to a sitting position, he heard Silver Chief whining softly.   Then he saw the dog leave his side and streak away into the darkness, the light from the dying fire gleaming on his sleek sides.   Jim tossed some more wood on the fire and as it roared high, Baker worked his way out of his robes, rubbing his eyes sleepily.

"What's the matter—wolves?" he demanded.

"I don't know yet."   Thorne was struggling out of his bag as he answered.   He reached down under his pillow for his clothes and was just about to thrust a leg into his pants when there was a rush out of the gloom.   The next thing Jim knew he was bowled back into his bag, fighting off the embraces of a small dog gone wild with the excitement of finding his master and his friend.   Mickey had caught up with them.

Silver Chief pranced proudly about the threshing figure of Thorne, waiting for the pup to finish his greetings.   But it appeared that this operation would take some time.   Snow, fur, thick paws, and fat body all seemed to move at once, tumbling down into the officer's sleeping bag, while the little red tongue licked at the man's face and neck.   A whimpering sound of joy accompanied this show of affection and the pup's heart beat as if it would tear itself out of the small, wriggling body.

At last Jim was able to get Mickey outside the sleeping bag, a bag that was by now soaking wet from

MICKEY HAD CAUGHT UP WITH THEM.

the melted snow carried in by the unexpected visitor. But Mickey was not half through with the ceremony. Another rush landed him on Baker's chest. The trapper, roaring with laughter, tumbled over backwards as he tried his best to ward off the frantic advances of the cub. Mickey didn't stay long with Baker. Thorne was his man, and soon he was back at him again, trying to claw and maul the big Mounty into pieces. At last with considerable effort, Thorne managed to set the pup down firmly on the snow. Then Silver Chief came in for his share of attention. With a glad, little yelp Mickey raced for him and sank his teeth into the big dog's leg. The Chief, as happy as his little friend, dropped to the snow to engage in a mock battle. His ears, neck, and tail all came in for their share of the tugging. Jim scratched his tousled head as he watched them. Then he pulled on his shirt, stoked the fire, and lighted a cigarette.

"Doesn't look as if we'd get any more sleep tonight, Baker." He grinned at the trapper who was busy trying to dust the snow out of the hood of his sleeping bag.

"How do you suppose the little devil found his way out here?" Baker wanted to know.

"I guess Meade must have let him out for a run, and he sure took one. That's quite a trek for the pup. Our trail's wide open. He couldn't miss it, but those stumpy little legs have been doing some traveling all the same. Well, he's here. I guess there's nothing for it but to take him along."

Jim was right when he said that sleep was finished for the night. The two men went back to their bags and soon the fire died down, but Mickey and the Chief had no intention of anything so dull as sleep. Nowhere in the camp would do for them but close to Thorne, and there they stayed, tumbling, grunting, squealing, and pawing, until the first gray shadows of dawn drifted through the timber. Jim roused from a sort of half slumber and realized that it was time to get under way.

Breakfast over and the teams harnessed, the most important problem was how to carry Mickey. Baker solved it. He took a small bag with a draw string, about the size of the one in which he carried bait. He punched two holes along either side through which he ran short pieces of lashing. Then he picked up the pup and shoved the fat, squirming body into the bag, tying the draw strings snugly just back of the dog's shoulders. He placed the pup on top of Thorne's load and secured the lashes on either side.

"He'll ride there okay," Baker remarked as he stepped back to view his work.

Jim laughed. "And he'll kick up plenty of fuss from that perch, too. Well, let's go."

As they glided easily away, the pup howled in terror at the swaying motion of the sledge. He kept up his protest for a few miles and then settled down to sleep. When he awoke, he seemed perfectly content and restrained his outbursts to occasional yelps. At each cry Silver Chief looked back from his place at the head of the team to assure his little friend that everything was going smoothly.

That day they finished traveling over Baker's line. The man pointed out to Thorne three different traps where he had lost fox. Strangely enough each of these seemed familiar to the big dog, and as they passed them, he whined and looked about inquiringly. At the end of the line the men swung south and were able to pick up Wright's territory before darkness forced them into camp. The following morning found them at the head of Howell's line.

"I can make out alone the rest of the way, Baker," Thorne said as they sat drinking their breakfast tea.

"I guess I'll stick along for today," the trapper answered. "We'll finish this one by nightfall and I'll start back in the morning. Then I'll leave you and head for home."

Mickey appeared from the bush, threshing through the drifts like a baby snowplow. He had picked up an old glove that someone had dropped along the trail and was tossing it proudly, stumbling over it frequently as well.   He brought it to the fire and squatted down to devote his attention to its destruction.

"When I get home," the Mounty laughed, "I'll have to tie down everything in the house.   Nothing is safe from that little guy.   He'd attack a kitchen stove without even waiting for it to cool off."

They finished breakfast and loaded the gear.   "Up you go, Mister," Jim said as he picked the pup up in his arms and tucked him into his bag.   Mickey made no protest this time but held fast to the old mitt, and spent the day chewing it.

They worked their way down Howell's line and across Swift River.   They found two or three fox in the traps and took them out, not wanting to risk wolves.   Also, Thorne reflected, wanting to prevent whoever it was that was robbing the traps from stealing them.   But the officer had to admit that the danger seemed small.   Silver Chief showed every evidence of being familiar with the territory.   At each trap Baker pointed out as the scene of a theft, the dog showed unmistakable uneasiness as if he had been there before. With the progress of the trip Thorne became more and more puzzled, and his anxiety about the dog increased.

Noon of the fourth day found them encamped on the south bank of Swift River, finishing some hot tea and warmed-over beans.   The day was brittle, cold, and sunless, and they crouched near the fire, holding the tea mugs in their mittened hands. The dogs burrowed into the snow for a nap, while Mickey dozed on the load, one fat paw clutching his beloved and sadly tattered mitt.

Baker tilted his head back to drain his cup. "You should pick up Big Rock sometime tomorrow morning," he said. "I don't think you'll make it tonight. Fifty miles is a bit of a job between now and sundown. Anyhow, you're not in a great hurry. I'll give you what's left of my caribou for dog feed, except for one ration. I'm going to push on into the settlement tonight."

"Don't answer any questions when you get there," the Mounty requested. "If they want to know what's going on, just say that the investigation isn't finished yet."

"Right you are."

They stowed their dishes and shifted the dog feed to Thorne's sledge. By one o'clock all was ready and, with a farewell wave, the trapper headed his team across the river and disappeared along the northern trail. Thorne gave his sledge a final tightening up and swung the team out onto the frozen watercourse. It would be a long afternoon's journey toward the two trap lines.

As he proceeded, the cold grew more intense. He could tell that the temperature was dropping, not only by the stinging of his nose and cheeks but also by the way the sledge dragged.   A light hoarfrost had appeared on the surface of the snow and the runners gripped.   The dogs had to labor now to keep the sledge moving.   From the top of the load Mickey began to whine.   The wind was nipping his nose. Jim stopped to turn the little fellow around and was rewarded with a quick lap of the small tongue.

As they got under way again, the Mounty began to chill through.   He increased his pace, swinging his arms against his body to stir the circulation.   At times he trotted a few paces ahead of Silver Chief, and the big dog, seeing him ahead, threw himself against the breast straps and pulled until his tongue dripped out the side of his jaws.   Jim saw that the sun was dropping over the tops of the spruce grove.   Another hour's travel, he decided, and they would hole in for the night.

At that very moment three startling things happened simultaneously.   A rifle bullet whined through the frosty air and ripped into the loose fur of his parka. The powerful jerk at his right shoulder spun him about so quickly that he dropped to the snow.   And blended with these came the cracking reverberations of a rifle shot, its echoes tossing back and forth in the silence like a small chip on the waves of a choppy sea.   As the officer hit the snow, he acted automatically.

With one twisting roll of his body he gained the shelter of the sledge. Reaching up, he grasped the "gee" pole and pulled with all his might. The sledge toppled over, dragging the dogs to a stop. Another shot whined. Again the echoes sounded, smothered this time in the screams of a dog, as Corky rose, twisted in the air, dropped to the snow, quivered, and died. Thorne worked fast. With one hand he yanked loose the lashings that held Mickey and dropped the pup down beside him. With the other, he pulled his rifle from its boot. Dropping his mitt, he pumped shell into the chamber. The cold steel stung his damp fingers but he paid no heed to it as he worked his way to the edge of the sledge and peered ahead of him.

A small cluster of rocks lay perhaps two hundred yards ahead on the right side of the river. Thorne knew at once that the shots must have been fired from there. He kept his rifle half raised, studying the spot of ambush. For fully ten minutes he watched, straining his eyes until the tears streamed down his cheeks. Nothing moved, nor was there any sound except the chop of the dogs' jaws as they bit ice chunks from their pads. Then very dimly he heard the creak of a swaying sledge far off behind the rock pile, and in a moment, the muffled voice of a man urging on a dog team. Again Thorne waited for long minutes but there was no further sound. Whoever had fired at him was not losing any time in leaving the country. Well, he would lose no time either.

With the first shock of surprise over, the Mounty felt a surge of anger. A police officer encounters many criminals in his work, but none is so despicable as the one who shoots in the back, who lies in ambush to kill in cold blood. Satisfied that his assailant had fled, Jim leaped to his feet. Quickly he righted the sledge and with his knife cut the dead dog from his traces. It took him some time to patch the harness and he swore at the delay as his chilled fingers fumbled with the stiff leather. At last it was mended. Mickey was set back in his place and made secure.

Then, rifle in hand, Jim stepped out ahead of the team. Despite the fury that smoldered in him, he was alert, tense, and calm. Ahead of him raced a treacherous killer ready to fire at the first advantage. This was to be a man hunt, and a fight to the finish.

VII

PURSUIT

THE rocks from which the shots had been fired were scattered about on a gentle rise that sloped back from the river bank. Farther inland the land was barren of any growth except an occasional small clump of willows near the feeder streams that slipped down from the highland.

Jim approached the ambush with the utmost caution. He felt reasonably certain that the person who had fired on him had driven away and that there was little chance of further shooting, but a plan of action which necessitated care in every move was already forming in his mind.

Nearing the rocks, he grasped Silver Chief's collar. "Whoa—boy—down—down," he said in a low voice.

The big leader looked up at the man and dropped obediently to the snow. The other dogs, surprised at the sudden stop without a shouted command, bunched up for a moment and then followed Silver Chief's example. Jim dropped to his hands and knees and worked his way slowly ahead until he reached the shelter of a boulder at the crest of the slope. From there he could see out across the Barrens. The marks of the sledge runners were plain, heading almost straight east. Way beyond, Thorne could make out the dark outline of timber against the horizon. For a long time he studied the whiteness. After a few minutes he saw the small figure of a man with a sledge team moving toward the timber. They were visible for only a second and then were lost behind a rise in the snow-crusted surface. Satisfied with what he had seen, Jim wormed his way back to the dogs and prepared to camp.

The world, always interested in the lives of men whose deeds are steeped in adventure, has coined a phrase about the Royal Canadian Mounted Police. "They always get their man." What part of the civilized world has not heard that ringing challenge? The Mounties themselves resent it, and every raw recruit at the training barracks in Regina is taught that he must never take that phrase literally. It has been abused, laughed at, and burlesqued in a thousand different ways until the entire force has come to loathe the sound of the words. Yet no truer words were ever said. They do get their men, even if the chase carries them to the ends of the earth, even if they must die in the search. And the main reason for this is the thoroughness with which they set themselves to the task of bringing in a criminal. Nothing is left to chance. Every move is planned and executed according to that plan.

So it was with Thorne. He was making his plans now before the chase, rather than blundering along without the proper preparation. He knew that a little more time spent at the beginning usually paid heavy dividends at the end.

Briefly, Thorne's idea was this. Whoever had taken those shots at him had not waited to see whether he was down. The dog's cry must have told the man that there was one hit, and firing at that range, both shots might easily have registered. Very easily, Jim thought as he fingered the torn hole in his parka. Reasoning further, it would be natural for his assailant to expect him to come rushing after him if he had not been hit. Therefore he would rest now and take up the chase after dark, thus allowing the fugitive to think he was in no danger of pursuit. Of course that meant giving the man ahead the advantage of distance and of being able to dig himself in, once he discovered he was being followed. But that, Jim figured, was a risk he had to take. For the time being he would stay here, have a bite to eat, rest the dogs a bit, and then start wheeling. The other man would have to stop sooner or later, his dogs would play out if he didn't, and Jim, with his dogs rested and fed, could keep right on after him. That meant that the Mounty should overhaul him about daylight.

Jim set about making himself as comfortable as possible. Mickey, who had been strangely silent all this while, was watching. The officer took the pup from his sack and set him down on the snow. Instead of removing the dogs' harnesses, he allowed them to rest where they lay. Mickey, free at last, pranced gaily up to the Chief. Jim took a little meat from the load and fed each dog. He kept the rations small because he didn't want the dogs to be sluggish when they got under way. For himself he took a tin of cold beans from the grub box and sat munching them with his back against the sledge. When he was finished, he stripped the sledge of everything but bed roll and food, even tossing off all the caribou except one ration. They would have to travel fast so that he could swing back into camp for food in case the chase took longer than he anticipated. Either that, or he would have to risk living off the land.

BACK OF HIM CAME THE TEAM.

Next he examined the rifle, the revolver, and the supply of ammunition. The revolver he strapped on beneath his parka. Then he lighted a cigarette and sat down to wait for the darkness.

It was early when he got under way, barely nine o'clock. Glancing back as he led the team up over the rise, he saw that the sledge was tightly lashed and shipshape, moving along easily now that most of the load had been removed. The darkish runner marks which Jim was using as guides showed up plainly, although there was no moon. Later when the moon came out, it would help him as much as the other man, as long as he didn't get into the timber. Watching the tracks, Jim came to the conclusion that the man he followed knew the country well, for his trail curved constantly, avoiding all the rough spots and only crossing slopes where it was absolutely necessary.

The cold was intense, the temperature much lower than it had been in the afternoon, but the pace set by the dogs kept Thorne moving so rapidly that only his face felt the sting of the frost. The night was quiet. The shuffling sounds of the dogs' feet, the creak of leather, the jingle of buckles, the soft whine of the runners rasped out on the frosty air with a magnified harshness. Thorne could hear the dogs breathing hard as they pumped the air into their lungs with

9

short gasps, and he marveled at the stamina and power of these huskies of the North.

The highland which Baker had described lay darkly to the left of the trail, and the Mounty wondered why the fugitive did not swing toward it for protection. Once in that deep bush, escape would be almost assured, and there would be the added possibility of being able to waylay his pursuer. But perhaps the man in front had had enough shooting and only wanted to put as many miles as possible between himself and anyone who might be following him.

Thorne speculated a great deal on the identity of the person he was pursuing. Who would want to put him out of the way? Of course there were probably many—men he had brought to justice and who might wish to revenge themselves against him. But they were all safely behind bars. Perhaps someone wished to get him because of the trap robberies. And yet that hardly seemed reasonable when it was pretty well established that a dog—his dog—was the thief. Besides even if Silver Chief were innocent and the thief a man, he would hardly attempt murder to halt the investigation. He would simply stop his activities for a while until the officer left the country. Thorne's thoughts went around in circles. Try as he might he could not get the thing to add up to any credible solution, so he put all these conjectures out of his mind

and concentrated on what he knew to be true. Someone had shot at him. He was on the trail of the killer
and he must bring him in. That was all that mattered
now.

Silver Chief was in his glory, for he knew that he
was in on a chase. The trail he followed still retained
the scents of man and dogs. More than that, he knew
that they were on serious business. Long hours on the
trail with Thorne had taught the dog the difference
between ordinary sledging and a man hunt. The gun,
the quiet voice, the speed of travel, the frequent stops,
all these meant that they were bent on something out
of the ordinary. And they meant, too, that Thorne
expected certain things of the dog—haste, attention to
orders, and faith in his master. With an occasional
look at Jim, the lead dog moved swiftly ahead at his
fastest gait, a pace which only the strongest could
maintain.

There is a theory that excitement engenders a sort
of toxin in the body which causes it to respond with
almost superhuman keenness and power. And it
would seem that dogs react in the same way. Whatever the cause, there was no denying the fact that once
on the trail in a man hunt, Silver Chief became as
alert as a human being.

The hours passed and still they pushed on relent-
lessly with never a sign of life ahead. At each isolated

grove of spruce, Jim halted the dogs and stood motion-less, rifle half raised, scarcely daring to breathe until he was certain that no threat lay hidden in the dark shadows of the trees.   Sometimes a load of snow would slip from a branch and land with a soft plop on the drifts below.   Then Silver Chief would growl and press against the Mounty's knee, searching the dark-ness ahead with uplifted head.   At these times Mickey would yip once or twice and then go back to sleep. After a little while they would move forward again. Before midnight a huge, golden moon swung into view, so big and so colorful that it looked unreal.   For a while after the moon came out, the tracks were more difficult to follow but as it climbed higher and its light grew more intense, the night became as bright as day and the visibility was perfect for miles.

The way the trail bore constantly to the east con-vinced Thorne that his quarry was headed for some sort of hideout.   The man was making no attempt to delay his pursuers, but seemed instead to be hurry-ing toward a spot where he could make a stand.   This made the situation more serious and Jim pressed forward at a swifter pace, hoping to overtake his man before he had a chance to barricade himself. Thorne thought of Indian Charlie's shack as a possible objective but dismissed the idea when he remembered that due to the illness of Charlie's brother, the line had

not been worked that far. It seemed unlikely, too,
that anyone except the inhabitants of Lake Caribou
would know of the existence of the cabin. And he
could not believe that anyone from the village had
fired on him.

After a while the moon sank low and then disappeared. With its going, one of the strange twists of
sub-Arctic weather set in. It began to warm up.

"Of all the luck," Jim grumbled to himself. "That
means snow, the one thing I don't want." With the
moon gone, the pre-dawn darkness came on, making
any further advance hazardous, so he stopped the team
to rest until daylight. His parka was frost-covered
and stiff, and the dogs' coats were so rime-covered that
they looked like shiny, silver blankets. Gratefully
they dropped to the snow for a few precious minutes of
sleep. Little Mickey, high on his perch, dozed
peacefully.

Thorne, puffing a cigarette, slouched against the
sledge and looked out toward the east where the
timber growth was beginning to be much more dense.
At times he fancied he saw a shadow moving stealthily
through the gloom. Once the illusion was so real that
he rose to his knees, his rifle ready to bring to his
shoulders. When nothing appeared, he realized that
his eyes were playing tricks on him after the long
strain of looking out across the whiteness. Satisfied

that no one was approaching, he sank back and continued his rest.

He couldn't help smiling when he thought of the position he was in. Here he was, a member of the Mounted Police, out to get his man, calmly sitting beside the sledge smoking. That would make a fine story if anyone knew it. Nevertheless he felt that his scheme was sound. That was where a criminal made his mistake. He committed a crime and then rushed for freedom, expecting the Mounties to make a swift dash in pursuit of him. But that was not Thorne's way. He had no intention of courting exhaustion and collapse unnecessarily. Rather he chose to harbor his strength and that of his dogs, picking up again when he had rested, to go on and on, to keep going on long after the one he followed was on the verge of dropping from fatigue.

With the dawn Jim moved forward once more. He was tired, dead tired. They had been on the trail twenty-four hours now and most of that time at top speed. His legs were heavy and he found it difficult to keep his eyes open. The dogs, too, were lagging. It was only Silver Chief's powerful tugging at the harness that kept them at a trot.

At seven o'clock the snow began to fall, blanketing the world in a silent shawl of gray-white with huge flakes drifting down so quietly that one might almost

SUDDENLY SILVER CHIEF STOPPED SHORT AND SWUNG HIS
HEAD AROUND.

think that a great feather mattress had been ripped open in the heavens. Jim soon realized that he need not fear the snow, for though the tracks they followed were completely covered, Silver Chief plowed ahead without once slackening his speed. He could not help marveling at the dog.

He was not moving forward blindly, weaving from right to left in bewilderment, but racing straight ahead and Thorne knew that the dog was following the trail even though he could no longer see it. Jim had heard of Eskimo dogs farther north doing this. There, when the men were lost out on a lake or the sea, they gave the dogs their head and let them lead the sledges back into camp. But this was the first time any dog of Jim's had done it. It must be the wolf instinct in the Chief, Jim decided, an instinct far more acute than that of any domestic dog. Whatever it was, Jim did not question Silver Chief, but let him go, contenting himself with keeping a lookout for any movement in the heavy snow ahead.

At last the timber became very thick and the drifts deeper. Suddenly Silver Chief stopped short and swung his head about to Jim as if he were uncertain where to go next. Jim peered carefully about him, soon discovering the reason for the halt. They had come to a trail, hard packed and old beneath the freshly fallen snow. Jim took the map from his pocket and studied it. This must be Lowe's line, he decided, since it was the first they had struck. Pocketing the paper, he let the dogs rest while he walked about on a tour of inspection. He stepped off the trapper's trail and moved toward the east, the direction in which he had been traveling. There was no sign of sledge marks, although he scraped away the snow in several places. Then he heard the sledge move, and turning back to it, he saw that Silver Chief had risen to his haunches and was hunkering along, sniffing the used trail and whining. That was enough for Jim. The Chief knew that their trail overlaid the one used by the trapper. After ten minutes' rest, they took it.

Through a silence so heavy that it seemed to press in on him, Thorne walked swiftly beside the sledge. Every tree, every bush, every snow-clad rock held a potential threat. Not for a moment could he allow his vigilance to relax. His legs grew heavier, his eyes burned and ached, but on he went. The dogs' traces slacked until they dipped into the snow, but each time this happened, the lead dog brought them up sharply. And still no signs of life nor any sounds except the creak and grind of their own gear and the labored breathing of the dogs.

It was warmer now. The snow on Thorne's parka melted and ran down inside his shirt, sopping it uncomfortably. As he walked along, he drew the wet garment off over his head and lashed it to a thong on the sledge. Mickey woke up long enough to shake off the snow, yawn, growl, and tumble back into another deep snooze. On Thorne went, knowing that if he did not overtake his man soon, he would have to stop and camp, for he was nearing the end of his strength. But he cheered himself with the thought that the man ahead must be tiring, too. Since there had been no evidences of a camping site along the way, the man must be racing top speed to some refuge. He would not be able to keep up his pace much longer, and then there would be a showdown.

Another hour's travel brought them out of the heavy timber and to the end of the trapper's trail. There Silver Chief swung without hesitation toward the east. Thorne could see no sledge marks but he trusted the Chief to follow without visible signs. As the day wore on, the melting snow sunk on the surface and once more the runner tracks stood out, proving the unfailing ability of the dog to cling to a scent.

The country was sparsely wooded and flat, yet as far as Jim could see, there was no sign of movement. Miles ahead the shadow of more forests glowered against the horizon. It was toward them that the tracks led.

They came to the first outlying fringe of spruce about noon. Jim, who had been walking along more asleep

than awake, forced himself to renewed vigilance. He
could see the Barrens, a vast flat stretch of land spread
out beyond the timber growth. Something inside him
gave warning that this was the end of the trail. As
if in answer to his thought, three shots in rapid succession whined over his head like the whirring buzz
of angry hornets. Before the last had sounded, the
Mounty dropped flat and took cover behind the sledge.
The shots were so wild that he concluded they must
have been fired as a warning. The dogs set up a
terrific yapping which told Jim that there were huskies
close by. He silenced the team and made them lie
down. Soon all except Silver Chief were curled up on
the snow, chewing the ice from their paws. The
Chief, however, lay with head turned toward the
timber, whining impatiently.

As Thorne's eyes became more accustomed to his
surroundings, he saw a small log cabin half hidden in
the woods. To the north side of the cabin the timber
was thick and tangled with a heavy undergrowth, but
the south and east were almost entirely exposed. It
was to the north side that he must make his way, not
only because it afforded him more protection, but
because it would cut off his quarry's chance of escape.
As things were now, the man in the cabin could easily
slip away through the timber and be gone for hours
before the Mounty missed him. If Jim commanded

that north position, the only remaining avenue of escape would be to the south in the open. But it was a problem how best to reach that shelter without exposing himself to fire.

Studying the situation, Thorne concluded that there was nothing to do but run for it. Speaking in a low voice, he managed to get Silver Chief swung about at right angles to the trail they had been following. After this maneuver he waited a few minutes, fully expecting a hail of shots from the cabin. But nothing happened.

"That's pretty dumb of him," the Mounty muttered to himself. "It's a hundred to one he doesn't even realize what I'm trying to do. Maybe this won't be as tough as I thought."

When all was ready, Jim rose quickly to his feet and called out, "Mush, Chief—mush, boy—hike—hike." Like a shot the big dog leaped ahead, dragging the others along at a breakneck speed. They were well within shelter of the trees when Jim pulled up, and not a shot had been fired. For a moment Jim feared that the fugitive might have slipped away from him, but this notion was to be disproved in the next minute.

"Halloa, there, inside the cabin," Thorne called from behind a log. "I'm an officer of the Royal Canadian Mounted and I command you to come out with your hands in the air. Do you hear me?"

In answer to Thorne's command a buzz of shots droned dangerously near. Well, that was that. It was to be a siege, with the cabin occupant holding all the advantages—warmth, food, and a chance to rest. The outlook was far from bright, and with a sudden desire to give vent to his irritation, Jim pumped five shots in rapid succession through the windows and doors of the cabin.

"That will let him know we can at least fire a rifle," he growled as he settled down to await developments. It was the beginning of a long and trying vigil. Evidently the man inside had no intention of letting the officer catch him napping, for at intervals of about fifteen minutes a few shots cracked through the air and thudded against the log behind which Jim and his dogs were crouching. The Mounty answered them to show that he, too, was still on the job.

As Jim studied the point from which the shooting came, trying to find a spot where he could place a bullet to good effect, he discovered a curious thing. The windows were not the place of fire. His own shots had broken two of them, and carefully as he watched, he could see no sign of movement in these openings. He had to admit that he was stumped. Once he looked up just as a shot was let go, and he was sure he saw a tiny flash near the base of the logs. That was strange. Were there holes so that the man inside could carry on the exchange while lying on the floor? Thorne fired a few shots along the edge of the floor logs and for some time there was no answer. Perhaps his deductions were right and he had scored a hit. But in a few moments a fresh fusillade told him that life, and a very dangerous life, still existed inside the cabin.

VIII

THE CAPTURE

AFTER the first few rounds of firing, the dogs, exhausted from the long trail, became accustomed to the noise and fell asleep. Even Silver Chief dozed a bit when things were quiet. Only little Mickey who had been loosed from his bag, stayed awake, yelping a protest to every outburst and trying in vain to lure the lead dog into play. Failing in this, the pup at last dragged his mitt up to Jim and settled down to the endless job of destroying the tough hide with his tiny teeth.

The day wore on slowly as Jim tried desperately to keep himself awake by munching pieces of dried meat and answering the shots that whizzed toward him at intervals.

Thorne had never before suffered so much from fatigue. It seemed as if he could not keep his eyes open. Every little while he would jerk himself upright with a feeling that he had slept for hours. The sun shifted around to the west and its warmth increased his drowsiness. He would have given anything he possessed to be able to stretch out, close his eyes, and sleep for hours.

Thorne was worried about the outcome of this siege for he knew that he could not hold out much longer. Sooner or later his head would drop down onto his chest and he would be lost in a deep slumber. Yet to rush to the cabin was asking for death. There was no hope of catching the occupant of the shack unawares. Nothing could be done but to hold on and hope for the best.

At about four o'clock something jerked Jim out of his fatigue-drugged stupor. Looking about him, he realized that Silver Chief had been growling for several minutes, his head eagerly turned toward the trail that they had covered the night before. Jim roused himself and looked in the same direction, trying to ascertain the cause of the dog's uneasiness. Spots moved before his aching eyes and he rubbed them hard, thinking he must be seeing things. In broad daylight, too.

10

Then he began to stare intently. He *was* seeing things but they were not illusions, they were real.

Far back on the trail two dog teams moved toward him, advancing slowly as if unsure of their procedure. Thorne came to his knees, but dropped quickly as a warning shot from the cabin whizzed past his ear. Lying prone on the snow, he called out at the top of his voice. The oncomers, close enough to hear him now, stopped and looked about, unable to locate the sound. Jim could distinguish the forms of the men. One of them was Lowe, but the other man he did not recognize.

At last they spotted Jim and waved. The Sergeant cupped his hands about his mouth. "It's Thorne," he called. "Leave your teams and come around through the bush. Watch sharp. There's shooting from the cabin."

The two men waved in answer and dragged rifles from beneath the load lashings of their sledges. Then they started in a roundabout way toward the timber. A few minutes later they were crawling on their hands and knees up beside the officer. It was Lowe and Wright. A tired smile creased the worn face of the Mounty.

"I never was so glad to see anyone in my life," he greeted them. "I don't know how much longer I could have held out. Keep down there, Wright, or you'll get potted sure."

Lowe squirmed in close to Jim. Wright took up his position at the butt end of the log where he could give the cabin a once-over.

"What's gone wrong, Thorne?" Lowe asked. "We came out to set some new traps on my line and we heard your shots."

Quickly Jim related what had taken place since he left Baker. "I don't know who it is nor what it's all about," he finished. "All I know is that he came close to getting me at the beginning and then beat it out across the Barrens. I've been right on his trail ever since and landed here early this morning to find him holed up."

"You know whose shack this is, don't you?" the trapper asked.

Thorne shook his head.

"Indian Charlie's," was the reply. "He took off from camp a few hours after you and Baker left. Of course he may not be in it now, but this is his place."

Jim considered this information for a time. "Indian Charlie, eh?" he said at last. "And fur stealing has been going on for weeks. Do you see any connection, Lowe?" he asked.

The trapper's cold eyes looked straight at Jim. "Yes, plenty. It looks as if I was wrong about Silver Chief, Jim. And I want you to know that I'm glad if I was. But we've got to smoke this bird out, whoever he is. More than likely we'll find this place full of fur and if we do, that will clinch the case. Charlie hasn't had time to do any more trapping than the rest of us and I don't think he's worked this end at all. If there's fur in there, it's stolen goods. Well, you're the boss here. What do we do next?"

"First, be careful." The Sergeant rolled over on his stomach and peered over the log. "The only way of escape is around on the other side and that leaves him wide open out there on the Barrens. Wright, you get over to the left about a hundred yards, and Lowe, you take the right wing at about the same distance. When we're all set, I'll give him another call and a chance to get out. If he doesn't come this time, we'll pour it into him until he does. Come on, now; let's get going before it's too dark."

The men wormed their way through the snow until they had reached their positions. Thorne, seeing that they were set, shouted for the man in the cabin to surrender.

"If you don't come out now, we'll come and get you," he finished.

Silence followed his request. Lowe called over his shoulder, "The beggar's asleep. Come on; let's rush him."

Before Jim could stop the trapper, he had raised himself to one knee. Instantly a shot rang out from the shack and Lowe plunged down behind the bush holding his shoulder.

"Hard hit, Lowe?" The officer's voice was anxious. Lowe did not reply, but in a moment Thorne heard him cursing softly. Jim smiled. No man who could swear with so much feeling was badly wounded.

"Nothing serious," Lowe called out finally. "But he plugged me clean through the shoulder. Whoever he is, he sure can shoot."

"You're telling me," was the Mounty's grim reply. "Watch out for fire from low down on the cabin wall. Don't waste any shots on the windows. You two hold on for a while. I'm going to feed the dogs and myself."

The two men signified their approval and Jim worked his way back to the sledge to get some meat. He tossed a piece to each of the big dogs and to Mickey and took out a can of beans for himself. Crawling back to the protection of the log, he began to eat and promptly fell asleep.

It was night when he awoke. At first he had trouble realizing where he was as he stretched out his cramped legs preparatory to rising. Then everything came back and he stayed where he was. He called to the two trappers.

"Nothing's happened," Wright answered. "We thought maybe you'd like a little rest. What do you think about rushing this outfit? There may be grub enough inside to hold us off for a week."

"That's just what we'll do," Jim replied. "You get back over here where I am and I'll tell you what I have in mind. Careful now that you're not seen moving."

It took Wright several minutes to make the shift without being seen, but at last he lay beside Jim. They moved to the far end of the log where Lowe could hear the plan of attack as Jim outlined it.

"I'm going to go back where Wright was. You two carry on here. As soon as I get set, I'll let go a couple of shots just as if we were keeping up appearances. That will be a signal for both of you to wham away. Shoot low, just above the snow line. Better take turns, first one and then the other. I don't know how that guy in there does it but he manages to cover all fronts. While you're keeping him busy, I'll move in. I don't think he'll spot me because he doesn't seem to be top-heavy with brains. I moved right around from the trail in full view of the shack and he never realized that I was getting under cover and cutting off his escape through the bush. I figure there must be another window on that south wall and if I can make it, the show will be over. How's that shoulder, Lowe?"

"Okay, but stiff as the devil. I've stopped it up with a handkerchief. It will do till we can take time out for a dressing."

HE STARTED ACROSS THE SNOW ON HIS HANDS AND KNEES.

"Good. Here I go. Let's wind up this thing." With that Jim crawled away into the darkness. Silver Chief rose to follow him, but at a word from Jim the dog sank back to the snow again.

It was perhaps fifteen minutes before a sound broke the silence of the night. The moon was low in the sky and the shadows of the timber lay like long, thin fingers against the walls of the cabin. Wright and Lowe were waiting for the signal. At last they heard a slight cough off to their right, followed immediately by one shot, and then three more in quick succession.

"Let's go, boy," Lowe called out as he took aim. He fired twice and then waited for Wright who followed up at once. Together they kept up a heavy bombardment at the small, yellow flecks of light which came spurting from the bottom of the cabin. The firing continued for nearly twenty minutes, the cabin giving back as good as it received.

In the meantime Thorne had not been idle. As soon as the shooting was well under way, he started across the snow on his hands and knees, stopping every few feet to sprawl out and fire. No return shots came his way and he made rapid progress around to the south side of the house. There he saw what he had hoped for, a window. Within about ten feet of the shack he rose to his feet and rushed the wall. Once there, he felt his way alongside carefully until he could peer into the room. At first the darkness of the interior made it impossible for him to see anything, but as his eyes grew accustomed to the gloom, he could make out a dim figure down near the floor.

The position of the figure puzzled Jim. Despite its nearness to the floor, it was not kneeling or lying prone, but judging from the humped-over appearance of the head and shoulders, appeared to be standing straight. And even more puzzling was the way it moved from one wall to another with incredible swiftness as it returned the fire of the two trappers. Gradually a thin slit of light bordering the wall in front of the man inside became visible and disclosed to the Sergeant the reason for the low firing. The chinking of the wall had been left out from between the lower logs and this space formed a perfect loophole.

Quickly Jim slipped his revolver from its holster. Watching until the man inside moved to the far wall to answer a burst which Lowe had sent into the shack, the Mounty crashed the butt end of the gun through the glass. Then he shoved the muzzle inside and covered the fugitive. The man turned in startled surprise just as Jim let go two shots aimed over the other's head.

"Drop that gun and stay where you are," the Mounty ordered. "I can see you plainly, so don't try any funny business." Then he called to the trappers.

"Okay, boys. Come on in." In another minute they had broken down the door. Wright flashed an electric torch into the room while the three of them looked about in amazement. Jim was the first to speak.

"Keep that bird covered until I can get in there and put the cuffs on him. I want to take a look at that room. That *is* something."

Lowe jumped down on a level with their captive and brought his gun to bear on the man's chest. "Come on in, Sergeant," he called. "I've got him."

Jim came around from the window to the door. As he entered, he heard Lowe call out in amazement.

"Well, I'll be hung. Guess who our boy friend is, Thorne? Indian Charlie himself. What are you doing here, Charlie, and what's the idea of taking pot-shots at people?"

Jim clamped the handcuffs on the Indian. "Take it easy," he interrupted Lowe. "Keep him covered. Say, did you ever see anything like this for a fort?"

The floor of the cabin was a dugout. Except for a square mound in the center, all the dirt had been removed from the interior to a depth of about three and a half feet. On the high point in the center there was a stove and a grub box, and against one wall a cupboard. That was all. No furs. No clothing or harness. Nothing except the trench, the stove, and the wall box.

"Sit down over there, Charlie," Jim ordered. "Wright, you go out and get my grub box and some wood. Let's cook up some food and coffee here before we do anything else."

Half an hour later the men shoved back their plates and lighted cigarettes. Thorne had loosened one of Charlie's hands so that he could eat, but the surly Indian, his eyes darting from one to another of his captors, had refused to say a word during the meal. So far Jim had not questioned him much, but now he tried to draw the native out.

"You'd better come clean, Charlie," he said. "You're the one that's been robbing these traps, eh? Well, where's the stuff cached?"

The Indian glared. "I have not stolen fur. You see it is not here. Your dog rob traps."

"He's probably stored the stuff away in the bunk his brother's been lying on sick," Wright offered. "Come on; let's look."

Lowe went over and shook his fist under the Indian's nose. "If you don't cough up what you know, you sneaking rat, I'll show you a way I've got of making people talk."

Jim pulled Lowe away from the Indian. "Easy there, Lowe. Keep your shirt on. I'm still in charge here. I'm going to take a look around for luck and then we'll move on into camp."

The shack was empty except for a half-filled tin of tea and a moldy package of oatmeal. Thorne took the torch and went outside. For a long time he prodded around in the drifts, but his efforts unearthed nothing. When he came back, his face was puzzled.

"People don't go around shooting just because they've stolen a few fox," he said as he sat down on the edge of the mound in the center of the room. "There's something queer about this whole thing and as long as this guy won't talk, we're stumped."

Wright was sitting on the trench opposite him. While Jim was talking, Wright's eyes had wandered to the bottom of the grub box behind the officer. For quite a few seconds he stared at the dirt in the corner of the box. Suddenly he slipped off the trench and ran across to the box. Charlie screamed and rushed toward the trapper, trying to strike at him with his steel-manacled hands. Jim floored the Indian with a short, stiff jab and let him lie on the dirt, cowering and trembling with rage, as he watched Wright's next move.

The trapper knocked the grub box off its perch and clawed at the sod. It came away easily. Jim flashed the torch on the spot, and Wright whipped out his knife and began to dig. The dirt came out in big chunks, and about ten inches down the blade struck something hard. Dropping the knife, Wright reached in and pulled out a tin box about a foot square, the sort used for packing biscuits. At the sight of the box, Indian Charlie swore and struggled to regain his feet.

"Watch him," Jim ordered. Lowe pushed the Indian down again and held his gun on him. Thorne handed the torch to Wright and took the box. Setting it on the floor of the trench, he pried off the top and looked at what he saw in amazement.

A bundle of money lay flatly folded across the top. Beneath this were many smaller packages, each wrapped in brown paper. Laying the money to one side, Thorne examined the contents of the packages. There were three watches obviously of great value. Another packet contained four diamond rings each with a good-sized stone. The others held a collection of cheaper jewelry, rings, bracelets, and cigarette cases. Thorne counted the money. It was in fives and tens and twenties and amounted to an even three thousand dollars. He put the loot back in the box and addressed the Indian.

"Where did you get this stuff, Charlie?" he demanded.

The Indian shrugged his shoulders. "I no see before. It not here when we build cabin."

Thorne turned to Lowe and Wright. "How long has this fellow been around Lake Caribou?"

Wright spoke up quickly. "He came in about a year ago last summer. He and his brother paddled down from somewhere in the North."

Again the officer spoke to the Indian. "Where did you come from? Where did you trap before Lake Caribou?"

"My brother and I, we been for years at Coppermine River, miles below the trading post at Coppermine. Before that we come from Great Slave Lake."

At this point Lowe broke in again. "He's lying, Sergeant. You know it as well as I do. Let's make him talk."

"Not here," the Mounty answered. He put the box under his arm and rose. "We'll wait until we get into camp before we do any more grilling. Right now I'm chiefly interested in sleep. That shoulder of yours needs attention, too, Lowe. Bring this fellow along and we'll make camp. In the morning we'll go on to the Post."

The trappers brought up their dog teams and shared the meat they carried with Jim's huskies. Thorne boiled hot water, cleansed Lowe's wound, and bound it with clean bandages. They arranged watches, Lowe taking the first trick because the pain in his shoulder would keep him awake anyway, and Wright volunteering for the last spell of guard over the prisoner. This allowed Jim to roll into his sleeping bag for the rest

he so badly needed.   The Indian, still handcuffed, was
placed near the fire, and the camp settled down for the
balance of the night.

Before the first streaks of light, they were up and
busy with breakfast.   After that they broke camp and
loaded the sledges.   Indian Charlie's dogs were turned
loose to follow them into camp, and the party got
under way.

As they sledged along, Jim Thorne puzzled.   He
had gone looking for stolen furs to help clear Silver
Chief's good name, and had found cached money and
jewelry.   There had been absolutely no trace of pelts.
He had a big job on his hands with his unexpected
prisoner before he really got to dig out the facts that
would prove the Chief innocent.

IX

ON TRIAL

IT WAS growing dark by the time they reached
camp. Doctor Meade, hearing the creak of harness
gear and the roaring bark of welcome sent up by the
camp huskies, peered out the window. In the dim
light he could see the little caravan making its way
toward the Post.

"It's Thorne," he said to Winship, who was busy
on his accounts. The Doctor hurried out to greet the
travelers while Dan followed him as far as the doorway.
The party came to a halt in front of the Post, and
Thorne, with the box under his arm, pushed Indian

Charlie ahead of him into the Trading Post room. Meade and Winship and the two trappers came behind him.

"What's all this about?" Meade wanted to know. "Don't tell me that Charlie's the one who's been stealing fur."

The Mounty did not answer. He took out the handcuffs and motioned to the Indian to sit down on a chair near the stove. One of the cuffs Jim snapped around Charlie's wrist and the other he looped through the back rung of the chair.

"Now you sit tight and keep quiet," ordered the officer. Then he turned to Wright. "Go and get this fellow's brother. You'd better take my revolver in case he saw us come in and tries to pull a fast one on you. And don't tell him anything. Say that Winship wants to see him."

"Are you going to need me for a while?" Lowe asked.

Jim shook his head. "Not tonight. You'd better go and have Mrs. Walters take a look at that shoulder of yours. The Doc will be here if you need him. And Dan will put your team away."

The two men went out. Winship passed cigarettes and then took a seat on the counter. "Now will you please tell us what this is all about, Jim?" he requested.

A slow smile spread across the Mounty's face as he leaned toward Meade who was holding a match for his cigarette. He drew a deep puff of smoke into his lungs before he answered.

"Well, my little tour of investigation turned out to be a lot more interesting than I looked for. No, I haven't anything new on the trap robberies—worse luck—but I did find out that some of the inhabitants of this little village are not in favor of having a Mounty around poking into things. In fact this guy was so disturbed that he took a couple of shots at me down on Swift River. When I finally caught up with him, here's what we found." Jim nodded toward the tin box on the counter. "Open it, Dan."

The manager took off the lid and pulled out the money and the packages. Meade looked at the stuff and then at Thorne and whistled softly. Thorne found a chair and went on with his story.

"Lowe and Wright happened along just in time. I couldn't have held out much longer because I was dead for want of sleep. If I had dozed off, this fellow would have nipped out on me, and the Lord knows how much trouble we might have had rounding him up again. Of course we would have had his brother, and I've a hunch they are both in on this thing. I want them both."

Jim's story was interrupted at this point by Wright who came in prodding a lanky, unkempt Indian in front of him. The Indian was thoroughly frightened and stood blinking at the men. Then his eye fell on the handcuffs that held his brother to the chair. A look of terror came over his face and he turned a sickly green color. He sought Indian Charlie's eyes pleadingly, but his brother met his gaze stonily and then looked toward the floor.

"What's this bird's name, Doc?" Thorne asked.

"Louie is the only one I know of," was the reply.

Jim tossed his cigarette into the front of the stove. Then he got up and took the loot from Winship. Walking over to Louie, he held it out in front of him. "Ever see any of this stuff before?" he demanded.

Louie looked at the money and the jewelry, and his lips quivered. He looked at Charlie but the Indian continued his same expressionless stare. At last, getting no clue from his brother, Louie shook his head.

"No," he grunted. "Not see before."

"Never seen it, eh?" Thorne persisted. "You didn't know we found it in your shack, did you? Had no idea it was there?"

Louie wet his dry lips and in a voice harsh with fear muttered, "We build shack over old cabin site. These things maybe there before."

Jim laughed shortly and turned back to the box. As he replaced the evidence, he spoke to Wright. "You may as well go along and take care of your team. I won't be needing you any more tonight."

Meade came up to Thorne. "How much is in that roll?" he inquired.

"Three thousand even. The four rings are worth at the very least two thousand more. The rest of the stuff is mostly junk. We'll have to locate the place it all came from."

Jim turned back to Louie. "Sit down there on the floor beside your brother." Then, "Wait," he commanded. "I'm not going to take any chances with you two." He pulled up another empty chair and placed it beside the one Charlie was sitting on. Forcing the second Indian onto it, Jim unlocked the handcuff that was attached to the back of Charlie's chair, passed it beneath a rung, and locked it around Louie's wrist.

Thorne turned back to Dan. "I'd like to take over that storehouse out in the back for a temporary jail. Clean it out, will you, Dan? And Doc, I'll have to ask you to stand by and keep an eye on these fellows while I put my team away."

Winship started for the storeroom. At the door he stopped. "Don't bother about supper, Jim. I'll clean out the room while you're gone and put Lowe's team away, and then get something to eat for the three of us."

"Okay," Jim said. "Food sounds good to me. By the way, how's that radio working these days? Do you get on at a regular schedule?"

"Yes, sir. They've finally come to realize that we are on earth and they keep open for us every morning and evening." Winship looked at his watch. "Seven o'clock is my night schedule. You've got half an hour. If you want a message sent, you'd better write it out and leave it here."

Jim went to the desk at the back of the room and sat down. Using the regulation yellow radiogram, he wrote out a message to the Mounted Police Headquarters in Ottawa.

J. R. Wilson, Officer in Command, Royal Canadian Mounted Police, Ottawa, Ontario

During recent investigation of reported trap robberies in this district was fired upon by trapper known here as Indian Charlie STOP pursued and captured him in his cabin where a quantity of jewelry including watches, rings, etc. together with three thousand dollars in cash was found STOP Indian Charlie and brother Louie have lived here for past year and a half STOP claim to have come down from Coppermine district and before that Great Slave Lake STOP advise any record robbery those locations past few years.

Sergeant Thorne

"Get that off as soon as you can," Jim requested the manager. "I'll be back after I've cleaned up a bit."

He went outside and started up the hill, calling Silver Chief to follow. The leader came to his feet with a bound and raced after his master, leading the team to the picket line in a flurry of snow. Jim unharnessed the dogs and gave each of them a generous portion of deer meat. Then he went into the cabin with Mickey and Silver Chief. He struck a light and placed food for his two pets in the corner. While they ate, he started a fire and set on a kettle of water to boil. As he waited for it to heat, Jim sat down on the bunk to smoke, realizing for the first time how tired he was from his long, sleepless watch. He would certainly get to bed early tonight.

When Thorne was bathed and dressed, he turned out the light and made his way to the Baker cabin. Baker and his wife welcomed him and pressed him to stay to supper, but he declined. Little Mildred was up and overjoyed to see Mickey again. Her father explained the pup's disappearance.

"I took him outside for a run and that's the last I saw of him. He trotted around the Store once or twice and then headed down your trail like a shot."

"Well, he's here again and I think he'll stay this time, Mildred," Thorne said to the little girl who was holding the wriggling pup in her arms. Even Silver Chief allowed the child to pet him. Apparently he approved of leaving the little dog with Mildred, for he went off beside the Mounty without a backward look. Mickey squealed once or twice when he found himself left behind, but with the talent which pups have for adjusting themselves to new delights, he pawed at the little girl in an invitation to play with him.

At the Store Jim found Dan at the radio tapping out his message. Meade was busy at the stove, and the two prisoners were not in sight. At Jim's questioning look about, the Doctor jerked his head toward the storeroom door and the key that hung beside it. Jim inserted the key in the lock and opened the door. The two Indians were crouched on the floor in the corner whispering together, but as the officer approached, they became silent. Jim asked them if they were warm enough, and they refused to answer. The Doctor had moved them in, chair and all. Jim took off the cuffs and looked around the room with satisfaction. It was perhaps twelve feet square and had no opening except a small window near the roof. Everything had been removed except a small box on which stood a kerosene lamp.

"I'll see that you get something to eat in a little while," the Mounty promised as he went out and locked the door behind him. Winship had finished on the radio and was setting the table.

"Going to have enough for those fellows, Dan?" Thorne asked.

The other nodded. "As soon as it is ready. I thought I'd feed them before we sat down."

"Good. And one thing more. Don't let me forget to take that lamp out of that room as soon as they've finished eating. That Charlie sure is a sly bird, and he might take it into his head to start a fire. Come on, Doc, hustle up that grub. I could eat a horse."

"Take it easy, Jim." The Doctor grinned at his friend. "The kitchen help around here only works at two speeds, slow and stop."

Thorne sat down for a smoke. "By the way," he remarked, "you seem to have increased the population since I left. What are all those empty shacks on the hill lighted up for? And I've never seen so many dogs or heard so much barking in my life."

"The Indians are here to trade," Meade explained, as he opened the oven and drew out a large caribou roast. "They come in about this time every year to get re-outfitted for the spring trapping and turn over what fur they have."

The Doctor cut two big portions of meat and placed them on a platter. He set this aside with bread, a pot of tea and two cups for the prisoners. Jim took the food into them, allowing each man only a spoon for eating utensils. Then he went back and sat down to his own meal.

"Pick up any leads on the trap robberies while you were out?" Dan asked as he reached for a piece of meat.

Thorne shook his head and neither of his friends pressed him further. After a while the Mounty said, "This is a strange case. It's what you might call open-and-shut against Indian Charlie, yet all we've got so far is the evidence without any proof of the crime."

"They're the last men in the world I would have suspected of being anything but two grouchy Indians," was Meade's comment. "What did Charlie say about taking a shot at you and how did he explain the dugout in the cabin?"

"He insists that when he saw me on the trail at one of Howell's trap locations, he thought he was firing at the thief who's been taking the fur. That's a hot one, isn't it? The cop out to catch the thief and he gets fired on as the thief. And when I asked him about the trench inside the hut, he said it was cold and hard to heat in the winter so they decided to use some of the stones from the river bank to build a foundation."

The two men smiled at the Indian's alibis. "A stone foundation on a trapper's shanty," mused the Doctor. "We *are* becoming up-to-date around here. They must have dug it out this summer. Did you see any of the dirt?"

"No. It was trenched out in the summer all right and the dirt hauled away. Oh, there's no doubt of their guilt in my mind. The question is where and of what. But we may know something when we hear from Ottawa. What time do you get on in the morning, Dan?"

"Usually about seven-thirty," was the answer. "I have to catch a few weather reports that clutter up the air for about twenty minutes before I can get my signals through."

Not long after supper was finished, Thorne rose to go. "I haven't caught up on my sleep yet," he explained as he yawned widely. He unlocked the storeroom door for a last look at his prisoners, and removed the lamp. Then he said good night to his friends and left for home with Silver Chief.

The big dog awakened him as usual the next morning and was let out to run while the Mounty dressed. Halfway through breakfast Mickey put in an appearance, having escaped the Baker home once more. Silver Chief looked the pup over and then lay down to submit to the inevitable maulings.

Jim had just finished putting away his breakfast dishes when Winship came in. He pulled off his gloves and helped himself to a cup of coffee. "Here's your message," he said, handing Thorne a yellow slip. "That ought to give you dope enough to hang those two babies." Thorne took the message and sat down to read it.

Sergeant Thorne, Lake Caribou, N.M.T.

Regarding Indians held as suspect, believe them to be identified with series of petty robberies, dance halls etc. occurring in Great Slave Lake district three years ago STOP later two Americans in Coppermine area on exploration trip found dead of starvation in cabin STOP no valuables found on bodies but families later testified each wore diamond ring and carried considerable cash STOP no record or measurements of men you describe but very likely traveling under changed names if they are connected with above crimes STOP proceed at your discretion to obtain conviction

J. W. Wilson
Commissioner

Thorne was smiling as he folded the radiogram. "That's the stuff I wanted," he told Dan. "I don't recall hearing about the cases they mention but I was in the bush a lot about that time and could easily have missed them. Come on, Dan, toss off that coffee and let's get going. Chief—parka. Parka. Gloves—Boy."

The big dog leaped up so suddenly that he sent Mickey spinning across the floor. Quickly he carried the parka and the gloves to his master and received his rewarding pat.

"Why don't you teach him to dress you?" Winship grinned. "It would save you a lot of time."

The two men and the dog went out, leaving the pup howling behind the closed door. Once at the Store, Jim worked fast. "Dan, run up and get Lowe, Baker, Howell, and Wright. And bring along anyone else that happens to be in camp. We're going to do a little grilling this morning."

He handed the radio to Meade. "These fellows had their breakfast yet?" he asked.

The Doctor nodded. Thorne went to the door and unlocked it, unfastening the flap of his revolver holster before he stepped into the room. He unsnapped the handcuffs, released the men from their chairs, and then snapped them together again by the wrists. He motioned them toward the Store, following them as they shuffled into the larger room. He placed two chairs in the center of the floor where they faced the light and ordered the Indians to sit down. The strong sun flooding in upon their grimy faces showed them to be even more worn and worried than they had seemed the night before. The Mounty sat down on the counter facing them. Neither he nor the Doctor spoke.

Soon Winship returned with the men for whom Jim had sent, and two or three others he had picked up along the way. Jim jumped down from the counter. "Let me have that tin box, will you, Dan?"

The manager went to the small safe behind his desk, while Thorne addressed the trappers who stood about the room talking in low voices and sending up great clouds of smoke from their pipes.

"We're going to have a little hearing this morning, boys," Jim began, "and I wanted as many of you as I could get to sit in on it.   Howell," he turned to a squat, red-faced man standing near the door, "you talk and understand this Chippewayan lingo, don't you?"

The trapper nodded and grinned.   "Yes, sir, Sergeant.   I ought to.   Been spieling it for ten years."

"Good.   You come over here with me then."   Thorne took the box and walked over to take his stand in front of the two Indians, Howell beside him.   He set the box on the floor and took out the packets of cheap rings and bracelets.   As he held them in front of Charlie, he said, "Take a good look at these things and tell me if you've ever seen them before."

The sunlight made the Indian squint as he leaned forward in his chair to look at the stuff.   After a moment Charlie looked up at Thorne and shook his head.   Jim turned to Howell.   "Tell it to him in Indian, so he'll be sure to understand."   But when Howell had finished a translation of the officer's words, Charlie still denied any knowledge of the jewelry.

"No lies now," Jim warned him.   "If you come clean, it will be a lot easier for you."   He replaced the packets and drew out the money and the rings. He tapped the fold of bills against his fingers as he watched the faces of the two suspects. "So you were in the Great Slave District, eh? Ever hear of some shacks and a dance hall being robbed there? And when you moved north, you didn't happen to come across a cabin with two dead white men in it, did you?"

Louie began to twist in his chair, his eyes glued to the money and the rings.

"Repeat it to them," The Mounty ordered Howell, and a rapid, guttural flow of words came from the trapper. As Thorne went on again, Louie became more terrified. "Those dead men had a lot of money on them, Charlie, but somehow when the rescue party found them, they were stripped clean."

Howell translated this, too, and as he finished, Louie turned suddenly to his brother and began to jabber incoherently. Charlie silenced him with a withering burst of words.

"What did they say, Howell?" Thorne wanted to know.

"Louie's scared, but Charlie told him to keep his mouth shut."

"Good. Now we've got them on the run. Repeat after me everything I say." Jim leaned over and shook the rings and money under Louie's nose, ignoring Charlie. "Never saw these things before, eh? Of course you didn't rob those two men and run away. You didn't come here and begin trapping and build a shack and dig out the floor, did you?" Howell repeated this, and Jim swung back to Charlie. "And you—you just go around shooting at people for the fun of it. Well, I've got the goods on you both, and if you don't come clean, I'll have to find a way to make you talk."

Thorne turned his back on the Indians. "Come here, Lowe," he ordered. "Take off your coat."

The lanky trapper stepped up briskly. He stripped off his coat and began to roll up his sleeves, eying the two Indians grimly. For a moment Louie's eyes darted around the room fearfully and then, as Lowe came toward him, he jumped to his feet with a scream of terror. The words poured out of him in a frenzied, meaningless stream. With a savage oath Charlie tried to drag his brother back to his chair, but Louie tore himself away and continued his outburst. At last he finished and fell back sobbing onto his chair.

Thorne looked at Howell. "It sounded like the works."

The other man nodded. "It was. Charlie wanted to bull it through, but Louie's nerve failed. It was a confession. I'll write it out for you and then read it back to them for signing."

"The furs, too?" asked Jim eagerly.

"No," answered Howell, "they confess to everything but the theft of the traps."

"That's all," said Jim curtly to the prisoners. "Get up." He led them back to the storeroom and locked them in. In spite of the elation he felt as a Mounty at the confession, he was sick at heart. For a heavy shadow still hung over the destiny of the Chief, a shadow the more ominous in view of the fact that the Indians had admitted more serious crimes, but claimed to know nothing of the pelts. With a grave feeling of depression Jim nevertheless hugged an odd kind of hope to his heart. He would tackle that job later. Now he must be contented with the gains of the moment.

When he returned from the storeroom-prison, he had to grin at Lowe. "You certainly took your cue well," he said. "What did you expect to do next?"

The trapper laughed as he buttoned the sleeves of his shirt. "I didn't know what you wanted me to do next, but I sure was set to scare the old Nick out of them. And I did, all right."

Thorne spoke again to the trappers. "I'm going to hold a public trial this afternoon here in the Store. All the Indians in camp will be brought in to listen, and I'd like as many of you fellows to be here as possible. And Howell, of course I'll need you again."

The men nodded their willingness to come, and as Thorne went out of the Store, they were all clustered

12

about the counter discussing the scene they had just witnessed.

The trial that afternoon was a strange gathering. The room, packed with men, reeked of sweat and rank tobacco. Indians with their squaws and children stood or sat on boxes. Most of the trappers and their families had jammed into the small room, too. On chairs in front of the counter sat the handcuffed prisoners, their glances shifting from familiar faces in the crowd to the floor, and back again.

Back of the counter sat Thorne and Howell. In front of the officer was a piece of white paper, the signed confession of Indian Charlie and his brother. They admitted several robberies in the mining district of Great Slave Lake and the robbing of the two explorers they had found dead in the cabin. There was no confession of any implication in the disappearance of the furs. Inwardly Jim groaned with uneasiness. The trap robberies were still to be cleared up, how he didn't know, though he was still bolstered by his lasting faith in the Chief. When the packed room would accommodate no one else, the Mounty rose, a striking figure in his red tunic, blue uniform breeches, and Sam Browne belt. Looking at him, it was easy to understand how a comparatively small body of men were able to keep peace in a territory covering hundreds of thousands of square miles. Thorne had called this meeting for the sole purpose of impressing on the Indians the power of the white man.   This was his first public trial, but years before, as a young, green constable, he had watched a grizzled sergeant of the old school do just what he was about to do.   Speaking directly to the two Indians, Jim began his speech, stopping after each sentence so that Howell could translate his words.

"It is for you to know that the King commands you, saying thou shalt not steal nor do murder. . . . Why does he command you so? . . . Long ago our Lord made this world. . . . He owns the world . . . the people also He made and them also He owns . . . the King of the land is commanded by God to protect the people, the white men, the Indians, the Eskimos . . . all these have the King for their ruler. . . . Therefore he has commanded them saying thou shalt not steal nor do murder. . . ."

There was not a sound in the room.   Only the two Indians stirred uneasily as Thorne went on.   "Now amongst you, two have broken this law of the King . . . they have stolen in a land far to the west of this camp and here they came to hide their deeds . . . but their deeds, being evil, have found them out . . . I am a servant of the King and I have found them out . . . therefore it is not for you or me to punish these who have stolen . . . rather I shall bind them and take them far away where they will stand before the judges

of the King . . . and should the judges find these two
guilty, then shall they be put away in the white man's
prison for many years where they can sin no more . . .
and where they may think about the evil they have
done and vow to steal no more . . . so I as a servant
of the King command you all to heed how evil is always
found out . . . how the white man's servant will not
rest until evildoers are taken and put away . . . I
command you to heed this so that you will think long
when you are tempted to steal or to do evil of any
sort . . . that is all . . . you may go."

Slowly the room emptied. The Indians went off to
their cabins very much subdued. Even the trappers
were impressed by Thorne's talk.

"It was a good idea," Meade observed as he stood
talking to a group before the fire. "These Indians are
impressed by a show, and Jim gave them a swell one.
I don't think there'll be any more trouble around here
for some time."

"How about the fur robberies?" one of the men
wanted to know.

Just at that moment Thorne passed the group on
the way to the storeroom with his prisoners. A
silence fell upon the men. Without a word the Sergeant turned the key in the storeroom door and hung
it on the wall. Then he walked through the room to
the door. "I'm dead tired, Dan," he said. "I think

I'll go home and hit the hay early. Good night."
And he went out into the darkness.

But tired as he was, sleep did not come easily to
Thorne that evening. Long after the dishes were
washed and put away, he sat before his fire and smoked,
reaching down occasionally to stroke the Chief.

Well, it was all over now. He had captured the
Indians and they had confessed to the robberies. But
he had failed to clear Silver Chief's name. He looked
down at the big dog who lay at his feet. Why did it
have to be his dog? Another man could have winked
at the law and gone away. But he, as an officer, must
mete out justice no matter how hard it might be. And
it was going to be hard. Somewhere Jim had read
that if you gave your heart to a dog, he was sure to
break it. Tonight that seemed almost possible—and
yet, as he went over in his mind, desperately, every
scrap and item of evidence, he gleaned from them just
one renewed conviction, that Silver Chief could not be
guilty, that he himself would bide his time, and that
he would be right.

Silver Chief shifted about uneasily, knowing that
his master was unhappy. He rested his head on
Thorne's knee and his eyes pleaded for the chance to
be of some help. Jim reached out and touched the
short ears, scratching behind them slowly. Assured
that all was well, the dog's jaws dropped open as if he

were laughing. Growling a little in his joy, he rose and circled the room in a prancing step trying to lure Jim into wrestling with him. When this failed, the dog looked quickly around the room and saw an old magazine on the bench near the bunk. He pounced on it gayly and brought it back to his master. Thorne could not help thinking of happier days—that long winter when he had lain in a lonely cabin with a broken leg and had amused himself for hours by throwing things for the Chief to retrieve. And he remembered, too, how, when he had tired of the game and had picked up his book to read, the big dog would carry on, piling everything he could reach at Jim's feet in the hope of more sport.

Thorne took the magazine from the Chief's jaws and held the fine head between his hands. He pressed his face against the smooth neck. But as he heard a whimper of joy deep in the dog's throat and felt the huge body quiver under his hands, Thorne rose and began to walk the floor. He could not bear to feel that body trembling with its silent allegiance of love and devotion.

Grimly the Mounty tried to tell himself that there was a way out. Yet he might have to shoot the Chief; then all his hope, all his convictions brought an inner certainty there was not. The men at the camp were watching him, waiting to see if he would flaunt his authority over two, poor, ignorant Indians and then allow his own dog to go free. He couldn't escape his duty, if, after fighting every inch of the way, the facts were proved. *But Silver Chief's guilt must first be proved.* Then, regardless of the pain it would cost him, he would do the thing himself. Another person might bungle the job.

Tomorrow or the day after that, if he had to, as an officer of the law, he would take his revolver and walk off into the bush as if nothing were going to happen. Then he would hold the dog around the shoulders—better that way than having to look into those eyes—and when he had a firm grip, let it go in the back of the head. That would be all. An easy matter of only a moment or so, and yet it would be the hardest thing he had ever done in his life. Up and down, up and down the small cabin Thorne walked, and as he went, the Chief's eyes followed him questioningly.

A sudden scratching on the door interrupted Thorne's pacing. With a welcoming whine Silver Chief raced to the door and stood waiting for Jim to open it. In pranced Mickey dragging his beloved mitt. Dropping it for a moment, he rushed at Thorne, trying to climb up the man's legs. Thorne rewarded him by rumpling his ears, then went back to his pacing about the room. Silver Chief romped with his friend for a little while but soon deserted Mickey to move anxiously after his master.

At last Thorne threw himself into a chair. Mickey dragged the mitt over to Jim and began his attack all over again. Silver Chief stretched out beside the Mounty. Jim could not get out of his mind the thought of what tomorrow or the day after might bring. And the loneliness of all the tomorrows after that. How he would miss the big, gray dog! No more walks in the woods with the Chief hiding ahead behind some bush, waiting to spring out at him with mock ferociousness. No more long evenings when he need only stretch out his hand to touch that loyal head. And never again on the trail would the big leader be up there in front fighting his way through the bitterness of the Arctic frost, fighting when all the rest of them were ready to drop from fatigue and hunger.

He lifted his head. "It isn't proved yet," he said aloud. Then once more dread overwhelmed him. By this time tomorrow night he might be alone. He would have walked out into the bush, the Chief trotting confidently along beside him. He would have done the job and returned—alone. He would have to take off his mitt to do it. Already he could feel the cold steel of the pistol trigger. It reminded him of the time Mickey's tongue had frozen to the ax blade, and how anxious Silver Chief had been as he and Winship

"What a Fool I've Been," Thorne Muttered to Himself.

worked over the little fellow. Yes, he would have to take off his mitt. Otherwise he might fumble. With a mitt on—mitt—mitt—mitt——

Jim was out of his chair like a shot to wrench the torn mitt from Mickey's jaws. The pup leaped back in fright and Silver Chief jumped to his feet in amazement at his master's sudden action. "What a fool I've been, what a fool I've been," Thorne muttered to himself as he examined the barely discernible bead pattern on the wet, slimy mitten. Could this be the needed proof of the Chief's innocence, right under his nose? It had been there for days and he hadn't seen any significance in it. For the mitt was the same, identically the same, as the one Indian Charlie had left on Jim's table the day he had forgotten the fox. And Mickey had picked it up at the junction of Howell's and Wright's trap lines. Indian Charlie could have been there for only one purpose.

With a whoop of joy, Jim jerked down his parka and gloves. He blew out the light and hurried outside. Impatient to be at the Store, he broke into a run with Silver Chief racing at his side and Mickey plowing along behind in a desperate attempt to keep up.

As Jim threw open the Store door, Meade, Lowe, Howell, and Winship who sat playing rummy, looked up in surprise. Thorne burst into the room like a human cyclone. Without a word he rushed to the place where the storeroom key hung, snatched it down, and opened the door. The next moment he dragged the two bewildered Indians into the light. As they stood in the center of the room, blinking at him, he waved the sodden mitt under Charlie's nose.

"That's yours." Jim made a tremendous effort to speak quietly, but there was iron in his voice, iron that bespoke no mercy for this man who was so nearly responsible for Silver Chief's death. "Don't lie to me about it," Jim went on. "You dropped it out near Wright's line while you were robbing his traps. And you used dogs while you were doing it so that if I went out there to investigate, I would find tracks and my dog would pick up the scent and make it look as if he had been there before." Thorne's voice was rising. "And you fed Mickey part of a carcass so the men would have some grounds for suspicion. And even though you're headed for prison anyway, you'd let an innocent animal die just because you hate me."

The Indian flinched under Thorne's angry eyes, but he said nothing. Jim reached out a brawny arm and twisted the man down onto his knees. "Tell them you did it," he shouted. "Tell them you're the one that's been robbing their traps. Not my dog."

Meade stepped quickly up to Thorne's side, afraid of what the Mounty might do to the Indian. But his concern was groundless. Charlie, groveling before

Jim, was confessing his guilt in a torrent of guttural sounds. "What does he say?" Thorne asked of Howell, who was best versed in Indian.

Howell answered: "He says, 'Yes, yes, I do it; I do it. I steal fur. I want they should think your dog do it.'"

With a laugh of triumph Jim loosed his grip on Charlie and turned back to the astonished trappers. "Did you hear that? There's your fur robber." He spoke to Wright. "You remember when the pup picked up this mitt?" The trapper nodded. "Well," Jim finished, "this is it, and like a thick-headed fool, it never occured to me till tonight that it was Charlie's."

Lowe stepped up to Jim with his hand out. "Thorne, we've been wrong," he said. "I want to be the first to admit it." And his hearty handshake told Jim that he meant what he said.

The officer turned again to Howell. "Ask them what they did with the furs," he commanded.

Howell engaged the terrified Indian in a round of rapid Chippewayan questions and answers. The trapper at last looked at Thorne admiringly.

"Seems it's a kind of compliment for you, Thorne. They got scared out of their wits and destroyed the furs. They say they would rather have been caught with the jewelry than with evidence of a false accusation against a Mounty's dog. News travels fast by a sort of magic in the North. After they robbed the traps, they got scared at the story of your tracking down Laval and lost their nerve."

Over in the corner Mickey sat beside Silver Chief, waiting impatiently for his master to regain his senses and give him back his mitt. Jim walked over to the pup and swept him up into his arms. He covered the little dog's face with his big hand and ruffled the short fur gently. Mickey squealed with delight and tried to gnaw at the heavy knuckles. Silver Chief, understanding that his master was no longer troubled, stood watching the two of them happily.

"Well, Chief," Jim Thorne addressed the husky. "I guess we win, after all. The furs were gone. There were dog tracks. There were no human tracks. But sometimes instinct—and faith—pay out. I knew you couldn't have made those tracks, and I knew that sometimes a man, with low cunning, can for a purpose conceal his own. If a dog's as fine as you are, Chief, he doesn't have to cover his tracks."

X

OUT OF THE BUSH

DOWN along the frozen watercourse of Big River the little party sped, sledge runners biting the brittle snow with a rasping whine, harness gear creaking in the frosty air, men moving swiftly and dogs trotting steadily.

It was late January. Thorne's job at Lake Caribou was finished. The little settlement was once again in good health, thanks to the untiring efforts of Doctor Meade and to Thorne's opportune arrival with the serum. There was nothing further for the officer to do, and he was headed out of the bush with his prisoners.

They traveled in open formation, a precaution against any surprise move on the part of the Indians. Charlie and his brother were first, each plodding along with lowered head, eyes fixed on the drifted ice. Hopelessness and dejection showed in every step, for they knew that each mile ahead took them that much closer to the end of their freedom. They walked abreast of each other but spaced about four feet apart, while Jim followed them a hundred feet in the rear. He knew better than to try any single file formation on this trek. At a sudden bend in the trail, one might dodge quickly behind the other and disappear in the bush, bringing delay and perhaps even disaster to the party. Jim had brought in prisoners before. He was somehow curiously reminded, for the second time since he had sledged into Lake Caribou with the vital antitoxin, of that other bitter trek across the ice with his half-mad prisoner, Laval, sledging ahead.

Clad in furs, the Sergeant marched with his rifle slung through the crook of his arm. The gun had been carefully wiped free of all traces of grease and was fully loaded, ready for instant use. His face was almost completely covered by the hood of his parka and the low, protective fur piece on his beaver cap.

Back of him came the team, Silver Chief maintaining a careful pace, not so fast as to overrun his master, yet brisk enough to hold the traces tight and keep the

huskies at their tireless gait.   A hundred yards back
of the officer's team, Baker's sledge brought up the
vanguard.   This was the supply unit, for Thorne had
deputized the trapper to accompany him on the first
leg of the trip to Eskimo Point.   Baker's load con-
sisted mainly of dog food, and it was his duty to maintain camp so that Jim could attend to the prisoners.
The food for the men rode on the first sledge, lashed
safely beneath Mickey.   The pup, after his first howls
of excitement at leaving the Trading Post, had given
up trying to attract any attention and had fallen
sound asleep in his makeshift sling.

The chill Arctic air was still except for an occasional,
"luk ou, luk ou, luk ou," as a flight of ptarmigan
waddled clumsily across the snow or drummed into the
air in frightened haste.   The sun shown dimly through
the heavy mist which hung in the air like a white,
wispy veil.   At thirty-five below, a swift pace was
necessary if men and dogs were to escape frostbite.
The tea stop had just been made, and it was a little
past noon, with five hours of hard travel ahead, before
they camped for the night.

It was the fifth day on the trail, yet their pace had
not slackened.   This was primarily due to Silver Chief.
The lead dog moved like a machine.   Big-footed and
heavy-bodied, he ran with easy action.   The front legs
snapped up at the knees and flipped forward quickly

while the hind legs drove stiffly ahead as if following grooves. The tail was high and well arched over his back, a sure sign that he was not tiring. Shoulder and chest muscles rippled smoothly below the short, powerful neck. As the dog ran, his head nodded a bit and his mouth was open as if in sheer joy at his own power. To keep ahead of him, Thorne was forced to drive the Indians to the limit. The first few days they complained bitterly about such speed, but after that they settled down and proved that they were good travelers. Baker, in the rear, was pushed to it to hold on.

Silver Chief permitted no lagging among the dogs. Hundreds of miles behind him had built them into a fast traveling team. He seemed to carry them ahead by his own power. They had begun to weaken just once, but in order to save themselves from being nipped on the hind quarters, they continued to fight on at the pace he had set without whimpering.

Their entire course lay down the river which flowed slightly south of east. Soon they would come to the Point, where they could rest for a night and take on new provisions. Then Baker would return to Lake Caribou, and Thorne would pick up an Eskimo at the settlement and head directly south out over the vast wastes of Hudson Bay.

They traveled in the customary silence of men who sledge the Arctic trails. At two-thirty Jim called a halt. The Indians dropped onto the snow for a breather as quickly as the dogs. Baker came up to Jim. Both the men's parka hoods were sheathed in rime.

"Don't know this country much, Jim," Baker said. "Is there good wood all the way along?"

The Sergeant nodded and looked up at the sun swinging southwest in a scarlet glow. "Yes, we can go on until dark," he replied. "We'll pick up my old camp grounds about fifteen miles down the river. It's high there and good wood."

After ten minutes they were under way again. And so they traveled toward the south with never a break in the pace, never a whimper from man or dog, and never a word to break the silence of the day's march. The teams were always halted near wood. Jim's first move was to bring his prisoners back to the sledge where handcuffs were snapped about their mittened wrists, and they were allowed to rest. Meantime Baker was cutting wood. By the time Thorne had unloaded the sledge and moved the grub and gear to a suitable place, fuel and sleeping boughs were ready. Then the trapper tended to the dogs while the Mounty started a fire and began supper.

Silver Chief, released from harness, spent a long time licking the ice from between his pads, while Mickey tumbled about him begging for attention. But the big lead dog was tired and needed rest, so with a gentle cuff the pup was sent along to bother another of the huskies.   The rest of the dogs were not always as patient as Silver Chief, and usually before the meal was ready, Mickey would come yelping to the Chief's side, nursing a nip administered by one of the weary sledge dogs.

When the dogs were staked out and fed and the sledges arranged for the night, food was next in order. While they waited for supper to cook, the two men removed their footgear and stretched it to dry before the fire.   The captives were fed first and then tucked into their sleeping bags.   These bags were bound around their shoulders with lashes so that they had plenty of freedom to move around inside, even though they could not draw out their arms.   Thorne was not worried about their trying to escape during the night. Dead tired from the day's run, they fell asleep as soon as they were trussed up for the night.

After supper Baker and Thorne talked a bit about the trivial occurrences of the day, smoked a pipe in the warmth and comfort of their sleeping bags, and then settled down for the night.   Silver Chief crawled close to his master and dropped into a deep slumber with Mickey curled between his folded legs.

Each day and night was much the same, varying only in degrees of coldness and brightness.   Savagely

At Last They Reached Eskimo Point.

bitter mornings found them up long before dawn preparing for the march. Their numbed fingers fumbled at the harness as they strapped the dogs into place. Then came warmed-over beans and bacon, washed down by long draughts of hot tea. And soon they were gliding smoothly away into the rosy flush of the east.

At last they reached Eskimo Point, where they were greeted with hot baths, hot food, and comfortable beds. Thorne engaged two Eskimos to go on ahead the next morning. They would prepare snowhouses and hunt food on the way. After a day's rest the Mounty said good-by to Baker, and the following dawn found him under way toward Churchill, four hundred miles to the south.

For the first time in many years he was riding, and was no longer forced to break trail or slog along beside the sledge. He was using the Eskimo method of travel, the long, narrow *komatik*, a sledge whose runners, made of frozen mud, glide across the ice like a skate blade. With the Indians in front of him and his gun close at hand, Thorne sat back in ease and left the job to Silver Chief, who padded along the fresh trail with the precision of a piston moving in its track.

Jim had many things to think about as he rode along, for there was an important decision to be made after he had delivered the Indians. His time was up with the Police and he was eligible to retire. Years of service lay behind him and the reward was his if he wanted it. Retire? The word sounded strange when he thought about it in connection with himself. He had heard it often during his years on the Force. He knew plenty of chaps who had retired and others who planned to, but somehow he had never thought about it as anything that would happen to him. It had always seemed so far in the distance, something that he associated with old age or physical disability. And he wasn't old. He had joined up when he was only a youngster and now he was in the prime of life.

To retire meant giving up the Force, the life that had been his for years, the only life he knew. What would he do with himself? To be sure there was the lovely little home beside a lake, high in the Laurentian Hills. Often he longed for it when he was on the trail. And there was someone who loved him very dearly waiting in that house, someone who made all the hardships and dangers worth while. But always before there had been that other life of the wilds waiting for him to come back, that life of freedom where a man could breathe and be his own master. He had never realized until this moment how much he loved that life and what it would mean to give it up forever.

He was young. And he had saved his money, too. There were plenty of things he could do if he resigned.

Not for a moment did Jim entertain the idea of retiring to a life of idleness. MacPherson at Winnipeg had been after him for years to come in on some mining development of his. It was sound, too. Mac was making money and holding a place open for him. Then there was always a political berth available for any ex-Mounty, but that prospect didn't appeal to Jim much. Still he needn't worry about finding something to do. There would be plenty of things. The point was should he retire? Over and over in his mind Jim turned that question as he slipped along the dreary miles toward Churchill. He would have to decide soon. Perhaps when he reached the Post, there would be word asking if he wanted his name placed on the Retirement List. Headquarters always wanted to know what their men intended to do.

The journey south was one of the easiest and most enjoyable that Thorne had ever made. The weather held fair and bright with fine visibility, just cold enough to make good sliding for the runners. His prisoners sat in front of him as stolidly as if they were carved from stone. Mickey yelped and chewed his mitt and slept while Silver Chief swept along in proud command of the sledge train.

The Eskimos did their work well. As the days lengthened, Jim drove until six or seven at night, and on calling a halt, would find camp already made and hot tea waiting. The Eskimos were good hunters, too, and had bagged three deer on the way down. They moved so swiftly with their big teams that they had time to drive inland for caribou. The snowhouses were well built and warm. When the dogs were fed and picketed safely away from those of the Eskimos, Jim would crawl into the igloo.

As he lay back on the sleeping bench, sipping his hot tea and smoking, he was filled with a sense of warmth and contentment. To add to his pleasure, there came to him the tantalizing smells of steaks and bannocks cooking over the fire. After a leisurely meal he would crawl between the robes and drop off into a restful sleep. It was far more comfortable in the little hut of ice blocks than sleeping in the open. Even the Indians seemed resigned to their fate and ate and slept placidly.

Seven days after leaving Eskimo Point, Thorne and his charges swept past the lighthouse at Beacon Cove and swung to a stop before the home of Corporal Murray, R.C.M.P., Non-Com., in charge at Churchill. The Corporal, short and stocky, his face flaming from windburn, stood waiting for them at the door.

Murray grinned as he came toward Jim with outstretched hand. "It's a long time since you've been in these parts, Sergeant," he said. He nodded at the Indians. "Who are your friends?"

Jim rose stiffly from the sledge and shook Murray's hand. "Just a couple of wandering boys with sticky fingers. Have my Eskimos come yet?"

Murray nodded. "Got in at noon. They're over at the Mission."

A slim, dark-haired woman appeared in the doorway. She smiled warmly at Jim as he came quickly toward her.

"Hello, Mrs. Murray," he said heartily, "can you take care of a traveler for a day or so?"

"Of course I can, Sergeant."

Many times in the past Jim's duties had brought him in to Churchill, and the Corporal's wife always treated him as if he were one of her own family.

Mrs. Murray spied Mickey. "Where in the world did you get that puppy? Bob, bring him here to me." Murray went to the sledge and released Mickey who was whimpering softly. The pup nearly wriggled himself in two as Murray handed him over to his wife.

She cuddled the soft, warm body in her arms. "He's a darling, Jim. I hope you don't think you're ever going to get him away from me."

Jim smiled. "Well, I don't know about that. He's a pretty fine little pup."

The woman ruffed Mickey's ears. "He certainly is a darling." She turned to Murray. "You go take care of the Sergeant's dogs, Bob, while I see about food. I'm sure he must be starving."

"Right, Marian. Come on, Jim, and we'll corral these two birds first."

The two men escorted Louie and Charlie to a small building off to the right of the Detachment House. Murray unlocked the door and turned on the light. The room was bare except for two cots and a table. The windows were heavily barred. Jim looked around with satisfaction.

"Perfect," he commented. "They'll be okay here."

"Sure they will," Murray agreed. "After we've had supper, I'll feed them. Come along now. Marian figured you would be showing up about this time and she's planned something special. Hungry?"

"I could eat nails."

They locked the door and went back to the dogs. It was short work for the two men to unharness the team and chain them to the spare kennels behind the house. They gave each dog a double portion of meat, and then with Silver Chief leading the way, they went back to the house.

To a man weary of trail food, Mrs. Murray's supper was a beautiful feast. As they ate, Jim told of his experiences at Lake Caribou. Later they sat in the cozy little living room before an open fire. Thorne stretched out comfortably in his chair, rolling Mickey about on the floor with his foot while Silver Chief watched gravely.

"This is the life." Jim's remark was accompanied by a genuine sigh of pleasure. "Bob, you've got a pretty soft berth here."

Mrs. Murray settled into an easy chair with her sewing. "He'll be appreciating it even more in another week," she said. "He's going out on patrol. I'll bet he'll wish for some of my biscuits more than once before he gets back."

The Corporal was passing cigarettes. "Right you are, my dear." He smiled at his wife and then turned back to Thorne. "You're up for retirement, aren't you?"

Thorne nodded and smoked in silence for a while. At last he spoke. "Yes, and it's a devil of a job to make up my mind about it, too. Sometimes I feel as if I'd jump at the chance. You know, when the going gets a bit rough, and you're half frozen and starved while you chase a couple of killers through the bush. Then you feel like chucking everything and turning in your uniform, and you wonder what on earth made you take such a lonely, thankless job anyway. But that's only temporary. Once you're back and have a good bath and some clean clothes, you forget all about the rough side and you know you wouldn't change jobs with anybody in the world."

"That's true, Jim," Murray answered. "But you've got to look ahead. You won't always be able to do fifty miles on the trail and get up and start it all over again the next morning. The old legs start cramping after a while and you can't take it the way you once could. That's the time to start looking around and ask yourself where you're going to wind up in this game."

Mrs. Murray spoke up. "And how about Mrs. Thorne and the youngster? It must be pretty lonely for her, Sergeant, having you away so much. They do send you out on the strangest trips."

"Yes, they're the ones to consider first," Thorne answered. "If I were alone, the answer would be easy. I'd stay on until they had to cut me out of my uniform. It's my job and I love it. But it's different with my wife and the boy to think of. Maybe I could wangle a Headquarters billet, but I'd be miserable in an office job."

Murray considered his friend for several minutes. He was older than Thorne, although he had not been in the service as many years. At last he said, "You haven't asked for my advice, Thorne. But would you like it?"

"Shoot."

"All right, here it is. Get out now, Jim. This is a young man's game. You've done your part, no one on the Force has done more, and it's men like you that have made the Force what it is. But the day is coming when you and I will be outdated and shoved back on swivel chairs whether we like it or not. The days of the trail and the dog team are nearly over. With flying developing the way it is, these young squirts will whip out across the Barrens and back in less time than it takes us to make camp now. And more power to them."

Jim nodded his agreement in courtesy to his host's opinion; but somehow, inside, he wondered whether he could ever really agree to a point of actual decision.

"Now's your time to leave," Murray went on. "You're not crippled as you might easily be. The trail can be a dangerous place. And you're not broke. You've got a splendid wife and son. Why, man, you've got the world by the tail. Take a good hold on it while you can."

Jim puffed at his cigarette. "You may be right," he said, rather grudgingly. "I hadn't thought about it just that way before. The world *is* moving pretty fast and the day will come when we can't keep up. But I think I'll take my holiday—I have three months coming and I'll think it over. I want to talk to Frances about it, too."

"What on earth are you going to do with those two dogs?" Murray said.

"Mickey can stay with us," Mrs. Murray offered. "Unless you have to turn him over to the Police."

Thorne smiled. "The little fellow is not one of the registered dogs of the Force. He just moved in and adopted me, so I guess I'll take him along. Donald will get a big kick out of him. The other chap came to me out of nowhere, too, and although he's entered on the books as one of the regulation sledge dogs, he's actually my property. I wouldn't dare show up at home without them."

"Does Donald know Silver Chief?" inquired Mrs. Murray.

"I doubt if he remembers him. You see he was only a little fellow when he was taken sick and I had to move the family south. They only come up here in the summer time. I don't think the boy would remember the Chief, although I brought him home a couple times when we were at Edmonton. But Frances does. She's the real boss as far as Silver Chief is concerned. When she's around, I don't rate."

"Well, you'd better send in your report and holiday request from here," the Corporal advised. "Turn the rest of your team over to me, and then take those two Indian beauties you've got locked up out there and get out. And don't come back in a uniform. Get into some kind of business. I'll be around in a few years asking you for a job."

A knock at the door announced company. There was Wilson, the radio man, and his wife, Craig from the Hudson's Bay Store, and Walsh, the Canadian Pacific agent. Mrs. Murray brought out cards and they played till midnight when she served them a lunch. Before Wilson left, Jim gave him two telegrams to send off in the morning. One was to Headquarters requesting permission to leave on his holiday and defer the question of his retirement till that was over. The other went to the little cottage by the lake. It said that he was well and would arrive the next week.

By noon the next day Jim had received the necessary permission for his vacation. He began immediate preparations for departure. There was train service out of Churchill only one day a week and Thursday was the day. That left him forty-eight hours to get ready. The most important task was preparing Silver Chief for the long journey to the East. It would be the dog's first ride on a train, and Thorne wanted to arrange everything so that the dog would be as comfortable as possible.

Silver Chief knew that something unusual was afoot. He and Mickey were left at home with Mrs. Murray much of the time while Jim hurried about the Post making the final arrangements for the trip. To be left behind was something Silver Chief did not understand, and he did not like it. He grew irritable and roughly repulsed Mickey's attempts to play with him. Of course the Chief had no way of knowing that Churchill was full of trappers whose dogs were running around loose, and Thorne did not want to risk any fights. Jim did not doubt Silver Chief's ability to take care of himself, but there was always the chance that the dogs might gang up on him. All Silver Chief knew was that he was being left behind, so he sulked about the house like a spoiled child and snubbed the puppy at every turn.

At last the great day arrived. Thorne fitted a leather collar about the dog's neck and attached it to a long leash. Silver Chief shook his head impatiently at this queer harness but he followed Jim docilely out of the house and across the snow. Excitement was on all sides of them, men moving rapidly about, men in small groups who shouted at his master as they passed. At last they came to a long, low building where numbers of people were standing about as if they were waiting for something.

In front of the building stood something that looked to Silver Chief like three long, black shanties with a lot of windows. He had never seen a train before. And in front of the three shanties stood an even stranger object, a huge and shiny monster that snorted great puffs of steam. The biggest moose Silver Chief had ever seen did not snort like this thing.

He advanced toward it doubtfully, pressing against
Thorne's knee, his hair bristling as he growled his
defiance.

There was noise and confusion everywhere, and once
the black monster spouted a sudden white stream
into the air with a loud scream. Silver Chief leaped
back and snarled, ready for the attack, but his master's
hand stroked him gently and his quiet voice assured
the dog that he had nothing to fear. Yet he was
afraid with the old, old fear of all wild creatures, the
fear of the unknown.

XI

HOMEWARD BOUND

IT WAS a queer-looking affair, this kennel that Jim was showing to Silver Chief. The Chief had seen lots of kennels before but none like this one with its slats across the back and front. His master led him gently to the opening and urged him by easy pushes to step inside. The front of the box dropped with a bang, and Silver Chief found himself looking out through the slats. There was hardly room enough for him to stand, and even when he lay on the floor, he was crowded. Fear rose up afresh in the dog, and it was only because Thorne and Mickey were standing

close outside that the big dog did not try to tear the
box to pieces.   Thorne kept on talking softly to him
and the pup raced round and round trying to get inside
while Silver Chief, shaking with terror, watched them.

That was the beginning of many horrible hours for
the big dog.   He felt himself being lifted.   The box
swayed unsteadily far above the ground, and when at
last they set him down, he was inside the train.   All
about him were strange odors, but strongest of all was
the man odor.   Men seemed to be rushing past him
like the startled caribou he had often chased on the
trail.   The noise was so bewildering that he could
scarcely hear his master's voice as Jim sat on the end
of the box and slipped a consoling hand between the
slats.   But this was nothing to what happened next.
First there was a terrific rumbling beneath his feet,
and when he tried to stand, he was thrown heavily
against the sides of his kennel.   It felt as if he were
moving and yet nothing looked as if it were moving.
The walls of his box did not move nor the walls of the
train.   For a long time the dog lay shuddering with
fright, but when he saw how Mickey pranced gaily
about on top of the box and how his master continued
to sit outside and talk to him, he began to grow more
calm.   At last he slept.

Later Thorne awakened him and gave him some
water and some food, but he had little appetite.

Always there was this odd sensation of movement that did not seem to be movement, and the rumbling under his feet was louder than ever. In the beginning it had made him a little sick but as this passed, he became resigned to his lot.

Occasionally the rumbling and the swaying stopped. Then the men inside shouted and rushed about once more. At one of these stops the Chief stood up and saw Thorne leading out the two Indians that had been with them on the trail. He whined and pawed at the wooden bars, straining his heavy body against them in his eagerness to go with his master. But in a little while Thorne returned with the Indians and fastened them once more to their chairs. Then Jim came to sit on the dog's box.

Hours passed, hours full of noise and dirt and darkness and the constant swaying motion, but still Silver Chief was not released. It seemed to be warmer now and when the wide door of the train opened, great bursts of fresh air swept in to cleanse away the odors of the room. Each time Silver Chief peered longingly out the open door, yearning to leap through the opening and be gone across the hills, to stretch his cramped legs in a dash that would carry him away forever from this terrible place. But then the door would close, and he was suddenly jerked off his feet as the rumbling began again.

At last the day came when the rumbling ceased for the last time, and he felt his crate being lifted and borne through the air. As the box came to earth, Mickey leaped at the bars in mad joy, pawing at the hands of his master who was trying to open the door. In a moment it was open and Silver Chief was free. As he ran about in the fresh air, he had never been so happy. Thorne slapped the dog's sides with affection, and the pup rushed about wildly.

Silver Chief ran ahead with Mickey to stretch his stiff legs, but soon returned to prance close to Thorne. Every few steps he paused to rear up against the man, his forepaws against the Mounty's chest as he felt the beloved hands rub his ears. Now that his first wild dash was over, his only thought was to be at Thorne's side and to avoid any further attempts to separate him from his master.

There were more people about than the dog had ever seen before, and there were many buildings, all much larger than the cabins back in the country from which they had come. The strange noises bewildered the dog, too, and there was confusion everywhere. Only the touch of Jim's hand on his neck as they walked along steadied him. After a few moments Jim stopped by another peculiar-looking object, black and shiny like the one which had carried them so far, but much smaller. Thorne opened the door and stepped inside, calling to the dog to follow him. Silver Chief hesitated, slowly put one paw on the first step, and at last came inside. Jim petted him and put Mickey down on the floor beside him. Another man sat in front alone. Thorne was talking out the window to a third man who stood holding the two Indians by their arms. After a while this man nodded to Jim and moved off with his two charges. Thorne called to the man in front, and again there was the sensation of moving, but this time Silver Chief was not afraid. Looking out the window, he could see things passing by, and a warm excitement tingled through the dog.

"Like it, Old Boy?" It was his master's voice and the dog looked up at him inquiringly. Thorne grinned at him. "I asked you if you liked the city, Partner."

Silver Chief did not understand although he struggled to associate the words with something he knew. Mickey, who had been bouncing from one side of the car to the other trying to see everything at once, suddenly gave up the attempt and pounced on Silver Chief. Happy to be free and filled with excitement, the big dog forgot how strange everything was and wrestled the pup to the floor where he proceeded to give the young scalawag the best-natured thrashing he had ever received. Then the dog lay contentedly back against Thorne's knee. Everything was going to be all right.

After a few miles the buildings appeared less frequently and Silver Chief could see off across the rolling hills. His nose tingled as he drew in the clean, crisp air. All the terrifying experiences of the past few hours were forgotten. Ahead of him lay a wonderful land, a familiar land, with snow and green timber patches and fresh, cold air.

The car swerved suddenly around a curve. Ahead lay a great stretch of ice which looked familiar to the dog. It was like the vast bay wastes or the small inland lakes he knew so well. The car turned off the main road and climbed a slight slope that led in among a thick clump of poplars. At the top of the hill was a large, low house, and here they stopped. Jim opened the door of the car and Silver Chief leaped out eagerly to sniff the snow. From the house came a loud shout and looking up, the dog saw a small figure running down the steps as fast as his short, fat legs would carry him. With a last joyous shout the little fellow threw himself into Jim's arms. Silver Chief was not sure whether he knew this child or not and walked nervously about Jim waiting for him to explain. With the boy still in his arms, Jim knelt down by the big dog.

"Here's Silver Chief for you, Donald," he said to the boy. "He's been with your dad so many years that I couldn't leave him behind. I've brought him home to you."

Donald Thorne was a stockily built child, blue-eyed
and fair haired. Grinning a slow, infectious grin that
made him look like his father, he thrust a fearless hand
into the furry neck of the big dog. Silver Chief liked
the touch of that small hand. He stepped closer and
thrust his long nose against the youngster's neck. His
master loved this little man. Silver Chief would love
him, too. The great head of the dog swung from father
to son as if to pledge his friendship for them both.

A woman was coming down the steps. Jim rose
quickly and went to greet her. Silver Chief remembered this gentle, brown-haired lady who smiled at
him so warmly and he went to her at once. He remembered her voice too, warm and caressing.

"You grand old boy," she said to the dog, taking his
head in both her hands. "Jim, why didn't you tell
us you were coming so soon? And how long can
you stay?"

Jim slipped an arm around her. "Don't know yet,
darling. A few months at least. I thought I'd bring
the Chief along to renew old acquaintances. But
wait."

In the excitement of arriving home, Jim had completely forgotten Mickey. The pup, hurt by this lack
of attention, had dropped to the bottom of the car, a
trembling little heartbroken bundle of fur. Jim lifted
him out and set him on the ground. With a whoop

Donald rushed for the cub and swept him into his arms. Mickey nearly turned inside out in his efforts to be all over the boy at once, and Donald laughed until the tears rolled down his cheeks. Jim and Mrs. Thorne watched for a while, pleased at the boy's happiness.

Thorne took his wife's hand. "Come along, Frances. This will go on for hours. I'm starved."

As they started up the steps, Silver Chief watched them and then looked back at Mickey and the boy. He was obviously not certain what he should do. His first impulse was to go with Thorne, and yet after a few steps he hesitated. This small boy belonged to his master and must be looked after, too. The big dog stopped and retraced his steps toward the youngster. Then he hesitated again and looked once again toward Jim for an answer. Jim was watching him with a smile but he gave no word of command to the bewildered dog. Finally the Chief sat down on his haunches and howled a plaintive call of distress.

"Poor thing." Mrs. Thorne had been watching him with sympathetic eyes. "Help him, Jim. He wants to be with you and yet he thinks he should stay with Donald."

Thorne held out his hand. "Come along, Boy," he said.

That was all the dog wanted, a command from Thorne allowing him to leave his new charge.

The days that followed were full of a wonderful new happiness for the little family. And of them all Silver Chief was the happiest. In the first few days' explorations he learned many things—that nothing about the smooth, rolling grounds was to be disturbed, not the chickens nor the pony nor the three cows that roamed the pastures back of the house. Nor were callers who came to the house to be molested or frightened. He took Donald in his charge and seldom let him out of his sight. This was a full job for Donald, and Mickey found new wonders to investigate nearly every minute of the day. And they went from one thing to another with a rapidity that kept the big dog busy trotting after them.

All day long when the weather was fine, the three of them wandered out of doors. And when snow or rain kept them inside, they romped in the playroom. A natural fearlessness of animals was deeply rooted in Donald and he handled Silver Chief as firmly and with as much affection as did his father. And the dog liked the lad. He understood that this small boy was the dearest possession of his master and must be guarded from all harm, but that was not all. The loving hugs the boy gave him a hundred times a day, the small hands ruffing his ears and stroking his fur, all these signs of affection made the big dog love the boy for his own sake as well as for that of his father.

So the happy days passed. Spring moved swiftly. The rain came and washed away the snow. Birds ventured back from the south and their songs filled the morning air. The strong sap mounted in the trees and tender buds pushed their way bravely into the world.

When the ice had left the lake, Thorne and Donald began to make plans for a great expedition to an island that lay deep in the timber growth far on the other side of the lake.

"We'll take Silver Chief and Mickey and pretend we're pirates that have captured the island from cannibals, eh, Daddy?" Donald spoke breathlessly one night at dinner as they were outlining their excursion.

"Righto, Son," Jim replied. "A few more warm days and we'll be off, pirates bold across the bounding sea."

Mrs. Thorne handed Jim his tea. "Speaking of bounding," she said, "when are you thinking of bounding back to your job? Or aren't you?"

Jim lighted a cigarette and leaned back in his chair. "What do you think about it, old girl? Would you like to have your husband stop being a cop?"

She looked at him with a soft tenderness in her eyes. "You know how I feel, dear," she answered. "I want

you to do the thing that makes you happiest. And I
know how you love that life. But Jim, I do get frightened sometimes—and so lonely."

Thorne rose quickly and walked around the table.
He put his arms around her shoulders and kissed her
cheek. "You've been an angel about it all these years
and I've been selfish, going ahead thinking of duty all
the time, almost perhaps more than of you." He spoke
quietly. "From now on you're going to have more
say in everything I plan—whether it means going or
staying."

"O Jim, I'm so happy."

Donald wasn't paying a great deal of attention to
his parents at that moment as Mickey had just walked
up to the table and calmly snatched a piece of cake
from his hand. But Silver Chief saw the two in each
other's arms. Contentedly he rested his head on his
paws and dozed.

One bright morning later in May, the pirate party
shoved off to seek the unknown treasures on Miser's
Island. They left amidst the gay farewells of Mrs.
Thorne and Rose, the maid, who had worked long and
hard over the picnic basket. Mickey, standing proudly
in the prow of the boat, barked bravely at nothing.
Jim rowed, while at his feet lay Silver Chief nervously
watching everything that went on and much perplexed by it all. Donald steered at the bow.

THE DOGS ROMPED ON THE BEACH.

They made their way in a leisurely fashion across the calm water, fishing as they went, and about noon they ran the boat up on the sandy beach of Miser's Island. The heavily timbered little island lay to the north end of the lake, about four miles from the nearest shore. Years ago Jim had built a cabin there for fishing parties, and the youngsters had used it for picnics from time to time. Quiet and cool and lonely, the place had a mysterious allure that made any visit to its shores an exciting event.

Jim and the boy unloaded the boat. Then, carrying the baskets and bedding, they made their way inland to the small cabin. The dogs romped on the beach, Silver Chief splashing knee deep in the clear water and Mickey following as far as he dared, returning in fright when the waves threatened to dash over his small head. At the cabin Jim and Donald set about unloading their boxes of supplies and preparing lunch. They had taken only staples, as they intended to camp out on the rocky, wooded hill behind the cabin.

"I want to do everything just the way you do it out on the trail," Donald said seriously as he staggered up under a load of cut stove wood. "We'll have supper over an open fire. Then we'll go off into the woods and stand guard all night. Then in the morning we'll hunt and explore."

15

"You make the program, Son," Jim said. "You're in charge on this trip. Silver Chief and Mickey and I are the crew and we take orders from you."

They washed down a lunch of bacon and eggs with hot tea. Then they made two packs, one with a light tent, the other with a few food supplies. And away they went into the mysterious country back of the cabin.

It was a wonderful afternoon. The big sledge dog remembered the days when years before he and his master had taken many strolls through the woods while Jim was recovering from an injury. Circling them, he ran ahead and, crouching behind bushes, leaped out at them. Then he was off again with the breathless Mickey tumbling after him. As the sun went down, they found a little grove near a spring and here they made camp. Supper was a grand affair, for as they ate, Thorne told the boy many exciting tales of his days on the trail. Later Jim propped himself comfortably against a log with the boy leaning against his arm. The dogs curled up close to them and went to sleep. The day's excitement had made Donald very drowsy. He reached up and put his arms around his father's neck.

"You're swell to me, Daddy," he said sleepily.

"I'm pretty fond of you, Son," Jim said with a smile. "In fact there's no one else in the world I'd rather hunt treasure with on my holiday. You see, your father is thinking of taking a rest from the Mounted Police and this will probably be his last assignment. It's great to be on a job with my own boy."

"Do you mind very much if your helper goes to bed?" Donald's eyes fluttered as he asked. Jim laughed, helped him to undress, and rolled him into his own little sleeping bag.

Toward five o'clock the next afternoon two tired but happy explorers made their weary way back to the cabin. The dogs, investigating something of vast importance that Mickey had turned up—probably a caterpillar—lagged behind. Don walked ahead of Jim and pushed open the door of the little shanty.

"Oh, boy, it's good to be home," he said as he slumped onto a chair. Thorne came into the room and dropped his pack. "Nothing like getting back to the base after a long trip, Old Timer," he said. "Now you take a rest while I smoke a cigarette. Then we'll rustle up some grub."

Jim lighted his cigarette and sat down, just as Mickey and the Chief came in. The big dog started across the room to his master, but in the middle of the floor he stopped dead still and raised his head. There was a noise at the window behind Jim, and then a voice.

"Sit still, Mr. Policeman." Jim turned to the window.

"Better not move," the voice warned. "You remember Laval, no? Well, I've come back the way I said I would when you send me away to jail. You——"

Silver Chief had wheeled at the man's voice and was about to spring.

"Stop that dog if you don't want him shot," Laval commanded. "Stop him."

Donald rushed to his father's knee. "Daddy, he's got a gun. He's going to shoot us," he cried out.

"Down, Silver Chief, down," Thorne ordered the dog. He slipped his arm about his son's shoulders.

"Yes, I remember you, Laval," he said quietly. "What are you going to do about it?"

The half-breed chuckled evilly. "First you will tie up that dog, Mr. Policeman. Then I'm coming in and we have a little talk. And it will be such a pleasant talk for you, see?"

XII

THE LAST ASSIGNMENT

BAPTISTE LAVAL tied Thorne to his chair and then, heavy revolver in hand, sat facing him. The outlaw was dressed in dirty, ragged overalls and a heavy blue shirt. He was unshaven and the coarse, black beard added to the evil expression of his face. He wore no hat, and his thick hair tumbled down over his forehead.

Donald stood beside his father holding tight to Jim's knees. His first fright had worn off and he faced Laval bravely, although the childish mouth quivered a little as he watched the ugly face of the killer who held them prisoner. Silver Chief lay in the corner of the room tied to a bunk post with a stout rope. The great dog had struggled vainly to free himself and now he lay stretched out on the floor, a snarl vibrating in his throat as he tugged at the leash that held him.

Mickey was confused by all these strange happenings. After watching Laval for a while, he galloped clumsily toward him in a friendly gesture of playfulness. His advance was met with a savage kick that raised the pup from the floor and landed him, squealing with pain, at Silver Chief's feet. Donald rushed at the Breed and beat at him with his small fists.

"Stop that, you. Stop that. He's my puppy and you can't hurt him."

Laval reached down and pushed the boy away so roughly that he reeled back to his father's side. Thorne, white with rage, tugged desperately at the ropes that bound him to his chair.

"I'll kill you for that, Laval," he said, his voice shaking with rage. "So help me, if you touch that boy again, I'll get free some way and kill you."

Laval threw back his head and laughed, his face alight with cruel glee. "But no, Officer, you will not keel Baptiste Laval. It ees Laval that will keel you. Ver' soon now, when she's get leetle darker, I take the small one and go away and we leave you here to, what shall we say—well, to t'ink about Baptiste Laval." And he laughed loudly again as if relishing the thought of these plans of his.

Thorne fought within himself to deal with the situation reasonably. He knew that he was confronted by a madman whose brain, fanatic in its hate for him, was nevertheless extremely clever in its murderous workings. To anger Laval too much would only bring added injury to the boy and to himself. Thorne could not guess what Laval planned to do next, but he was sure that if they were to escape his insane plan, their one hope lay in delay. Time was the only ally Jim had and he sought to utilize it to the fullest. He steadied himself until he felt that his voice would not betray his emotion. Then he spoke.

"I don't know why you are doing this, Laval, or what you intend to do next, but don't you realize how foolish you are? You can't get away with it. Suppose you do kill me. What will that get you? They'll find you wherever you hide. They'll find you if a hundred men die in the chase. And when they track you down and bring you back, you will die, too. You're not scaring me at all. All I ask is that you let the boy alone."

Laval fumbled in the pocket of his shirt and brought out a foul-looking pipe. Without taking his eyes off Thorne, he produced a match and drew deep breaths of the tobacco smoke into his lungs. Then he leaned forward.

"So the Policeman don' know why Laval ees here, eh? Dat ees ver' funny. You remember me, no? You remember when you chase me halfway across Canada 'cause someone say I keel Swede trapper up Nort'? You remember you tak' me prisoner when you have broken leg, and hol' me wit dat dog all winter, den drive me like sledge dog into camp? You no remember, Mr. Policeman, dat you lash me wit whip when Baptiste ees tire and fall down? And when we get to camp, I am send way to Stony Mountain Prison?"

Laval spit into the corner of the cabin and wiped his mouth off on his shirt sleeve. "Well, I remember all dem tings ver' good. I be in dat prison now t'ree years. Nobody dere suffer like me. I t'ink and t'ink how it was all fault of yours. Now Laval do a little pay on what he owes you."

"I brought you in because it was my job to do it, Laval, and you know it," Jim snapped. "When you broke my leg by shooting at me from ambush, I had to make you wait on me. On the trail you tried to quit and I had to drive you. If I hadn't, both of us would have frozen to death. We nearly did as it was. As for the killing charge, that was up to the magistrate, and I've no doubt you deserved what he gave you. How are you going to fix all that up by harming me or my son? You'll just have to take it all over again, only this time it will be worse."

Laval smoked on, grinning at Thorne's words as if they amused him. "I don' care much if I die so long as I pay you up," he said. "All dees time in prison I plan it. Den at las' come my chance. The guard she ees changing and I knock one out and tak hees keys. I go out dat gate jus' like free man. It ees fine joke on cop, no?"

Laval stopped and rocked with laughter at his fine joke. Then he went on. "Den I find out where you live and come here for your boy, but den you come home and mak t'ings so much de better. Now don' you worry, Mr. Policeman, 'bout dat boy of yours. He ees fine boy and I no harm heem. Only he come wit me. It will be only short time till I hide across de line. After dat dees countree which hurt Baptiste Laval pay plenty money to get your boy back. He won' be hurt——only——" Laval chuckled maliciously, "you no know dat. You no know not'ink any more."

The Breed knocked the ashes from his pipe and stepped to the window. It had grown dark and the wind had begun to stir through the trees. The murmur of the lake lapping against the beach came through the stillness of the dusk.

Donald put his arm across Jim's shoulders. "What's he going to do, Daddy?" The boy's voice betrayed his fear.

Jim tried to reassure him. "Nothing to you, Son. Just do as I tell you and everything will be all right. Don't try to fight against him because then he may hurt you. Keep cool, old boy, and we'll get out of this yet."

Laval walked back to the table and held a match to the kerosene lamp. He sat down and lapsed into a scowling silence. In the corner Mickey forgot his hurt and began to gnaw at a piece of rope. Silver Chief lay quiet but hate raged in him like a mighty torrent. He recognized fear as all dogs do, and he knew that fear was in the heart of the man who had come into the cabin, despite his brave talk. Once before this same man had hurt his master, and now he was trying to harm not only Thorne but the boy as well. Every inch of the dog's body throbbed to be at the man's throat, to rip and tear at the hated body until it dropped lifelessly to the floor. Straining at his ropes, he snarled menacingly at Laval.

The Breed turned to the dog and grinned. "Dat's right, old dog. You growl while you can. You remember Laval, too, eh? Well, Laval he got some t'ings to pay you, too. Pretty soon you won' growl no more den I be even wit' you, too."

Ten minutes passed. Ten interminable minutes in which Thorne considered every possible way to outwit Laval. He measured the distance to the man with the hope that he could tumble forward in his chair and upset Laval. Then if he could roll him across the floor toward the Chief, all would be over. Once the Chief had gripped him, Thorne could get the upper hand. But Laval stayed at a safe distance from him and was constantly on the alert. Donald watched the man, fascinated in the terrible way that a small animal is fascinated by a snake.

At last Laval rose and went to the corner of the room. He picked up a five-gallon can of kerosene and removed the cap. He found a cup and filled it with the oil.

Jim struggled to rise. "Don't do that, you fool. You can't set fire to this place."

Laval snarled angrily. "I can't, eh? So Policeman t'ink he can still tell Laval what to do. Well, dis time Laval he do de talking. You watch."

With a quick toss he splashed the oil against the log wall. Again he refilled the cup and again he dowsed the cabin. Nor did he stop until he had the whole of one side dripping. Then he dropped the can and stood in front of the Mounty.

"Good-by, Officer. We go now and you won' never be bothered no more."

He snatched Donald from Jim's knee and swung him into his arms. The boy screamed and fought and kicked until Laval's open hand smacked the little fellow's face with terrific force. Donald's head fell back on the outlaw's shoulder, and he sobbed brokenly.

Jim, his muscles nearly bursting in his attempt to free himself, shouted hoarsely at Laval. "Stop that, Laval. Don't take the boy. Leave him alone outside and do what you will with me. But let him alone."

Laval paid no attention to Thorne's outcry but went on out the door with the boy. After a moment his face appeared in the open window. He was laughing now, and Donald lay quietly in his arms, apparently too numbed by fear to struggle any longer. Laval dug into his shirt pocket for a match. Calmly he lighted it and held it against an old newspaper. When the sheet was in flames, he tossed it into the corner where the dry moss and wood offered ready fuel for flames. The fire licked out hungrily into the oil-soaked logs and burst into a steady glow. Then the man at the window disappeared.

A feeling of absolute helplessness surged over the Mounty. All the time he had sat there, tied to his chair, he had been certain that something would intervene to save them. But now that all hope had vanished, he felt strangely resigned and calm as he watched the fire race eagerly along the oil veneer of the logs.

Well, this was the finish, he thought, and what an ignoble finish it was to be. Sitting here waiting to be burned alive was not the way Thorne had expected to end his career as a Mounted if it were to be the end. Give him a gun and a good stand-up fight and he'd take his chances on whatever fate had in store for him. But to die this way, tied to a chair, without even a chance to defend himself or the boy, was no end for a man. He gritted his teeth, wishing for the greater risks—and greater chances—of the North again.

Laval was crazy, but his plans had been laid with the cunning of the insane. Undoubtedly he had a boat concealed somewhere on the island in which to make his escape. Sooner or later the flames of the burning cabin would be seen from the shore and they would send help, but it would come too late. Already the fire was beginning to roar before the steadily rising wind.

It was hot now. The sweat stood out on Jim's body, and the heat of the flames seared his face. Mickey, puzzled by the fire, galloped to the center of the floor to watch. Then, frightened, he yipped loudly and raced back to Silver Chief. The big dog was on his feet tugging against the rope that was knotted around his neck. He had swung his body so that his back was toward the flames as he sought to draw the noose over his head. Thorne watched him without interest for a moment, then he realized that the dog was fighting for his master as well as for himself. New courage rose in Jim, and with new courage, a sudden idea. He began swaying his chair back and forth, further and further, until at last his weight toppled it over and he fell to the floor.

The entire wall was alight now, a roaring, crackling barrier of red-hot flame. It was unbearably hot within the shack. As he writhed across the floor, Jim's clothes began to smolder. Mickey howled in terror and rushed to the door but he would not desert his friends. Silver Chief pulled harder than ever.

Coiling himself like a spring, Jim bumped along as best he could toward the fire. It was slow, heartbreaking work, but the dog's courage in the face of almost impassable odds had inspired the Mounty to one last attempt at escape. Inch by inch he succeeded in getting his body turned so that his back was next to the fire. With a last jerk he edged close enough so that he could feel the fire against his ropebound wrists.

The pain was terrible. For a moment he thought he would faint, but he bit his lips and shoved his body a bit closer to the red-hot wall. If only he could endure it until the fire had burned the rope through. The pain shot through him like lightning, and he felt himself slipping into unconsciousness. He tried to fight against it but he no longer seemed to have any control over his mind. Just at that moment Silver Chief plunged through the air toward him. The rope had parted where Mickey had been chewing on it, and the dog was free. Jim felt the dog's face close to his and his arms loosen as the rope gave way. He rolled over on his face trying to fight back the nausea that swept over him. Silver Chief continued to bend over the man. When Jim moved a bit, the dog raced to the door, but he was back again in an instant. Thorne struggled to a sitting position and nudged the rope down off his legs with hands from which most of the flesh was burned. That was enough for the Chief. His man was alive and moving again. But there was still work to be done. The dog turned and raced out into the darkness.

The trail was plain. It led back to the far side of the island. There was no moon, but the fresh scent that Laval had left lighted the way for the dog. With incredible speed, the long, gray shadow glided across the rocky hills, head low, tail straight out behind him, every sense attuned to night sounds and the man odor that was strong before him. Through a patch of timber it led, then down a long slope to the water. At the lake's edge it ended.

Silver Chief investigated the beach carefully and at last picked up the scent once more. It led off in two directions and as he was about to turn and follow the stronger of the two, he discovered the reason for the division of the trail. A rowboat lay on its side amid strewn rocks along a narrow bay. The boat was battered by the waves and a gaping hole showed through the bottom. The man odor was strong here and then went off along the beach in the general direction of the cabin. Padding softly, the lead dog trotted along this new trail.

He must have traveled twenty minutes before he heard sounds in the darkness ahead of him, the soft sobbing of the boy, followed by deep guttural words of anger. The waves were rough on this side of the island and they splashed against the dog's belly. He moved inshore a few feet and increased his speed to a gallop. In the darkness he could make out a long, black object riding on the water. The bulky outline of a man stood at one end of the boat, straining to get it afloat. Suddenly the dog heard Donald scream.

"Silver Chief. Silver Chief. Here, Boy, here!"

There was a hoarse shout as Laval wheeled. Just as Silver Chief gathered himself to leap, a flash blinded him and he felt a hot stinging pain in his shoulder. Like an answering bullet, he hurled himself through the air and his long fangs clamped into the soft flesh of the man's leg.

Down they went together, threshing wildly in the shallow water. The first time his head went under, the dog's breath was jerked from his lungs and he released his hold. Laval scrambled to his feet and rushed for the boat. Silver Chief came to the surface and plunged after him. Laval raised the oar and brought it down across the dog's shoulders. The Chief was dizzy and weak and he could taste blood in his mouth, but he lunged again, this time floundering against the side of the boat where Laval stood with the oar. Again and again the blows fell on the dog, and slowly he released his paw hold on the boat. With one last mighty heave, he lifted himself and closed his jaws about Laval's ankle. Then he fell backwards dragging the man with him.

As the water closed over Silver Chief's head, he heard Donald cry out and heard from the shore his master's answering shout. Then everything was black and he seemed to be sinking into a bottomless pit.

*   *   *   *   *   *

Jim hobbled around the corner of the whitewashed stable holding his heavily bandaged hands carefully before him. Mrs. Thorne, her hand under his arm, aided him in his first tour outside the house. Donald walked ahead, talking rapidly.

"And he's going to be all right, Daddy. Doctor James says so. Doctor James brought another doctor down from Montreal and they stayed with Silver Chief three days while you rested in the hospital.   Now all he needs is a long rest, too, and he'll be good as ever."

"I'm sure he will, Son," Jim replied.   "He's too tough an old soldier to die.   Where is he?"

"Right over here by the wall.   I've fixed a soft bed for him in the sun."

They walked slowly along and soon the three of them stood looking down at Silver Chief.   The big dog was lying on his side, held in that position by a broad strap.   His foreleg was in a rough splint, and his shoulder was bandaged.

As the dog looked up at his master, his soft eyes seemed to melt with love and tenderness.   Thorne leaned down and rested his hands on the smooth head as he spoke softly to the dog.   They had been through plenty of the rigors and adventures of the North, the two of them, plenty of pretty tough scrapes together. Dimly Jim Thorne felt a surge of a strange kind of homesickness.   Did the Chief, too, feel it?   Was there somewhere in that majestic canine head a loyalty to the Mounted that made him also feel "once a Mounty always a Mounty"?   Jim wondered about a problem that only time could solve.

"We won't decide it now, Chief," he said.   "But perhaps we shouldn't be settling down just yet.   If it's the trail again for us, you'll be ready, too—eh, what, old fellow?"

At his master's pat, Silver Chief's tail stirred slightly, but the great dog did not try to rise at that moment. Broken ribs are painful.

Mickey romped around the corner and greeted them all with a yelp of pleasure. Hurl'ng himself in front of Silver Chief, he licked at the big dog's paws. Then he set to work nibbling on the splint.